"If we decided to get married, how soon do you think…?"

Dana didn't need to finish the sentence. Jared had already thought through their marriage of convenience.

"As soon as possible," he said firmly. "I don't receive the money from the trust fund until I have a marriage certificate."

"Of course, it wouldn't be a real marriage." Dana gave him a questioning look. "I mean, you can't expect me—us…"

Jared bit back a groan. Oh, he wanted her all right, and if she were honest, she'd admit she wanted him, too. The two times they'd kissed diminished any doubt of that. They'd been nothing less than explosive. "To consummate the marriage," he finished for her.

She nodded as a blush covered her cheeks.

"Dana, if you're worried I'm going to jump you, I'm not. If you want to take the relationship further, I'll leave that up to you."

Dear Reader,

The summer after my thirteenth birthday, I read my older sister's dog-eared copy of *Wolf and the Dove* by Kathleen E. Woodiwiss and I was hooked. Thousands of romance novels later—I won't say how many years— I'll gladly confess that I'm a romance freak! That's why I am so delighted to become the associate senior editor for the Silhouette Romance line. My goal, as the new manager of Silhouette's longest-running line, is to bring you brand-new, heartwarming love stories every month. As you read each one, I hope you'll share the magic and experience love as it was meant to be.

For instance, if you love reading about rugged cowboys and the feisty heroines who melt their hearts, be sure not to miss Judy Christenberry's *Beauty & the Beastly Rancher* (#1678), the latest title in her FROM THE CIRCLE K series. And share a laugh with the always-entertaining Terry Essig in *Distracting Dad* (#1679).

In the next THE TEXAS BROTHERHOOD title by Patricia Thayer, *Jared's Texas Homecoming* (#1680), a drifter's life changes for good when he offers to marry his nephew's mother. And a secretary's dream comes true when her boss, who has amnesia, thinks they're married, in Judith McWilliams's *Did You Say...Wife?* (#1681).

Don't miss the savvy nanny who moves in on a single dad, in *Married in a Month* (#1682) by Linda Goodnight, or the doctor who learns his ex's little secret, in *Dad Today, Groom Tomorrow* (#1683) by Holly Jacobs.

Enjoy!

Mavis C. Allen
Associate Senior Editor, Silhouette Romance

Please address questions and book requests to:
Silhouette Reader Service
U.S.: 3010 Walden Ave., P.O. Box 1325, Buffalo, NY 14269
Canadian: P.O. Box 609, Fort Erie, Ont. L2A 5X3

Jared's Texas Homecoming

PATRICIA THAYER

THE
TEXAS
BROTHERHOOD

SILHOUETTE *Romance*®

Published by Silhouette Books

America's Publisher of Contemporary Romance

To Tyler
My buddy, I'll miss sharing my office with you.

To Hence,
Your knowledge is invaluable to me; so is your friendship.

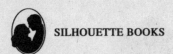 SILHOUETTE BOOKS

ISBN 0-373-19680-6

JARED'S TEXAS HOMECOMING

Visit Silhouette at www.eHarlequin.com

Printed in U.S.A.

Books by Patricia Thayer

PATRICIA THAYER

has been writing for the past sixteen years and has published seventeen books with Silhouette. Her books have been nominated for the National Readers' Choice Award, Virginia Romance Writers of America's Holt Medallion and a prestigious RITA® Award. In 1997 *Nothing Short of a Miracle* won the *Romantic Times* Reviewers' Choice Award for Best Special Edition.

Thanks to the understanding men in her life—her husband of thirty-two years, Steve, and her three grown sons and two grandsons—Pat has been able to fulfill her dream of writing romance. Another dream is to own a cabin in Colorado, where she can spend her days writing and her evenings with her favorite hero, Steve. She loves to hear from readers. You can write to her at P.O. Box 6251, Anaheim, CA 92816-0251, or check her Web site at www.patriciathayer.com for upcoming books.

All underlined places are fictitious.

Prologue

He only came back because of his brother.

Jared Trager Hastings stepped into his father's office. The musty-smelling room looked dull and gloomy with its dark-stained paneling and opaque drapes. The heavy oak desk and chairs were the same pieces his grandfather had used years ago.

With his brother, Marshall's, death, Jared knew that he had just moved to the head of the line to take over the family business, Hastings Development. That was never going to happen. Jared had always been a major disappointment to his father, unable to live up to Graham Hastings's high standards. Marsh had been the perfect son. Now he was gone, dead at thirty-one from leukemia.

A strange numbness claimed Jared. Two brothers couldn't have been more different—one doing everything to please his father, the other doing whatever possible to alienate the man, including running off at twenty. The one regret Jared had was that he'd missed knowing his brother. Now it was too late.

Jared checked his watch. He needed to get on the road. It was a long drive to Nevada. Suddenly the door opened and Graham walked in, along with Marsh's wife, Jocelyn. She was slender to the point of looking frail. Her dark brown hair was pulled back in a bun and her eyes seemed too big for her face, but she appeared to be the one helping GH into the room.

"I thought you'd be gone by now," his father said.

Graham had aged rapidly. At fifty-nine, he easily looked an extra ten years older with his deeply lined face and thinning gray hair. Today, his back was bent and his gait shaky.

Jared refused to let the man rile him. "You asked me to stay so we could talk."

"Since when did you care what I wanted?"

"Like you ever wanted me around," Jared threw back.

"Please, no fighting today," Jocelyn pleaded. "Marsh wouldn't have wanted this."

Jared felt ashamed. "I'm sorry, Jocelyn."

She nodded her appreciation. "I'm the one who wanted you to stay, Jared. To tell you how grateful I am you could be here today. If we could have gotten word to you sooner—"

"Hell, boy," Graham snapped. "Your own brother was dying and no one knew where the hell you were."

Jared clenched his fists to keep from saying anything. He turned to his brother's widow. "You were saying, Jocelyn?"

She looked at her father-in-law. "If you'll excuse us, Graham…"

"As if anyone here cares what I want…." the older man grumbled as he walked around his desk and collapsed into the chair.

Jocelyn went to a far corner of the room and Jared

followed. "I need to give you something." She spoke in a hushed voice as she reached inside her purse and drew out an envelope. "Marsh wrote you a letter just days ago." Her dark eyes filled with tears. "Jared, your brother struggled with himself for a long time, but he felt you deserved to know some things."

Jared tensed. "Know what?" He took the envelope from her and began to open it.

Jocelyn stopped him and glanced at his father. "Not here. When you're alone, read it." She released a long breath as if a weight had been lifted off her. "Marsh wasn't perfect. He made mistakes like all of us, but I loved him." She brushed the tears from her cheek. "And I know it gave him comfort to be able to say what he had in his heart. He did love you, Jared."

Jared took the letter, then he pulled his sister-in-law into a tight parting embrace. Unable to speak, he nodded his goodbye and left.

Later, sitting in his truck, Jared opened the envelope. There were several papers clipped together. On top was Marsh's letter.

Jared,

I know it has to be strange to hear from me like this. It's been a long time, and no one is sorrier than I that we lost touch. I used to think if things were different, maybe if Mother had lived, you wouldn't have left home.

I've always envied you, Jared. You never felt the need to live up to the rigid Hastings standards. You set your own. Of course it's easy now to look back and see our mistakes. And I've made many, which leads me to what I have to say.

Nearly six years ago, while going through Mother's

things, I discovered a picture and an old letter that led me to San Angelo, Texas, searching for a man named Jack Randell. A man that our mother once loved. I never found Randell. I located his family, but decided not to pursue it any further. I regret that, because in my search I discovered things…many things you have a right to know. Please, Jared, read the letter.

There's more to the story. While I was in Texas, I fell in love with Dana Shayne. I didn't stay because I was to marry Jocelyn, a choice I've never regretted. But I recently learned I'd fathered a child. I'm thrilled, but I regret that I'll never be able to see my son, Evan. So I'm asking you to go in my place. I've set up a trust for the boy so he'll be taken care of. But he needs to know his family.

I know it's a lot to ask, but please, Jared, don't let Father in Evan's life. I'm afraid of what he might try to do if he learns about him. You can't let GH ruin another Hastings.

Also, San Angelo just may have some answers for you, too. I'm sorry I'm not around to help, but read Mother's letter. It explains a lot of things.
Always,
Your brother,
Marsh

Jared couldn't believe what he'd read. He ran his hand over his face, not surprised to find tears. Marsh had a son. A child he would never know. With a shaky hand, he reached for the yellowed envelope addressed to Audrey Trager, opened the flap and took out the single sheet of stationery along with a picture. It was a younger version of his mother.

Dressed in brightly colored Western clothes, Audrey Trager wore a rhinestone crown on top of her blond hair. The white ribbon draped across her had the bold lettering, Western Days Rodeo Queen 1971. Next to her stood a tall man dressed in jeans and a Western-tooled shirt. He had dark hair, partly covered by a large black Stetson. Grinning at the camera, he had Audrey pressed against his side.

On the back of the photo, was written, "Audrey Trager, Western Days Rodeo Queen, and Jack Randell, bull-riding champion." Jared then unfolded the single piece of paper that had only one paragraph.

Audrey,
   I'm sorry to hear your news, but I told you from the beginning that all I could give you was a few good times. Now it's time I move on. As for the baby, you're on your own. Guess I forgot to mention I'm already married. So you might want to get rid of the kid.
Jack Randell

Jared's heart pounded in his chest as he reread the paragraph that suddenly changed everything. He checked the postmark, six months before his birth date. Damn, he wasn't Graham Hastings's son. That explained so much. The man's anger, the resentment…the hatred. Jared glanced down at his fisted hand and the crumpled letter inside it.

So he'd been passed off to one bastard by another. To another man who didn't want him. As if he had a choice about who his father was. It didn't sound like Jack Randell was any better at the job.

But that didn't stop Jared from wanting to find out the truth.

Chapter One

She was doing this for Evan's sake.

Dana Shayne dreaded the trip into town, but it had to be done. She closed the door to the house and walked down the porch steps with her four-year-old son in tow. Evan's dark, wavy hair was neatly combed for a change, and his best jeans and striped T-shirt had been freshly laundered. On his quickly growing feet, he wore his black-tooled cowboy boots that Bert had taught him—to her dismay—to spit-shine.

Her son looked up at her. "I saved my 'lowance, Mom. Can we get ice cream?" he asked, using his best, how-can-you-resist-my-face? look. Then he added a few blinks over his chocolate-brown eyes.

Dana doubted they'd have anything to celebrate today, but she wouldn't deny him the simple pleasure of an ice-cream cone. "Sure we can, honey. That sounds good."

She opened the door to her daddy's old 1970 Ford crew cab truck and helped Evan into the safety seat in the back, then went around to the other side. She checked her gathered print skirt and white short-sleeve cotton top. Already the late-spring weather caused her to perspire, and today of all days she needed to look cool and confident. The last thing she wanted was for Mr. Wilson at the bank to see her sweat.

Dana started up the truck and headed toward San Angelo. Passing the Lazy S Ranch sign that her granddaddy had put up years ago when he'd settled in West Texas, she suddenly felt sad. How much longer would a Shayne own this land? This had been her and Evan's only home. How could she leave it? But since her father's death, she and the sixty-five-year-old foreman, Bert, couldn't handle the place alone, and not many ranch hands would work for what she could afford to pay.

Dana had hoped to expand the cattle operation. Maybe if she had done it a year ago, she'd be able to pay the upcoming balloon mortgage payment. But there wasn't enough money. As if on cue, the truck hit a rut in the road and she groaned. So many things around the ranch needed fixing, not just the road, but the roof on the house and barn, along with most of the fencing.

Dana sighed. Somehow she had to convince the bank that if they lent her more money, she could make a go of it.

"Hey, Mom," Evan called from the back seat. "I'm gonna get pep'mint."

Dana smiled and turned to her son. "Peppermint sounds good. I think I'll have that, too." She couldn't believe how fast her baby had grown. He'd soon turn five, and this fall he'd be heading off to kindergarten. No doubt the separation would be tougher on her than her son.

A horn sounded and Dana turned back to the road only to discover she had wandered into the path of another vehicle. With a gasp, she jerked the wheel to pull the truck back on her side. Overcompensating, she ended up going off the shoulder and into the high grass. The truck bumped and bounced but she managed to keep it under control until it finally stopped. That's when she heard the screech of tires, followed by a crash.

With her heart beating like a drum, Dana managed to put the truck in Park and unbuckle her seat belt. She turned around to Evan. "Are you okay?" Her hands were shaking as she reached for him. She caressed his face, trying to soothe his fears.

"Mom, that was scary."

She saw the fear in his eyes and his trembling lip. She stroked his arm soothingly. "I know, honey, but we're okay." She didn't want to remove him from his safety seat, not until she checked on the other vehicle. "Mom needs to check on the people in the other truck. So you have to stay here."

The child nodded. "Hurry, Mom."

"I will," she promised as she climbed out of the cab. Her legs were weak, threatening to give out, but she gathered her strength, knowing someone could be seriously hurt. She raced across the deserted two-lane road to the late-model Chevy extended cab with Nevada plates. With the new highway, hardly anyone used this road, not unless they were coming to the Lazy S. Seeing the bent hood and hearing the sound of steam from the radiator, she knew there could be serious injuries.

"Oh, God, please, don't let anyone be hurt," she chanted as she ran to the driver's door and found a man slumped against the wheel. When she jerked the door open, he started to lift his head and groaned. That was a good sign, wasn't it?

"Wait! Don't move, you could be hurt."

"If a devil of a headache counts, I'm dying."

Dana watched as the man raised his head all the way and turned toward her. He had thick, raven-black hair and deep blue eyes. He had at least a day's growth of beard, but not enough to hide the cleft in his chin. She didn't see any sign of injury or blood.

"Do you hurt anywhere other than your head?" She examined his broad shoulders and his chest covered by a denim shirt. Her gaze moved down over long, muscular legs encased in faded jeans. On his feet he wore crepe-soled work shoes, instead of the area's standard cowboy boots.

"No, and if the air bag hadn't gone off, I'd have been fine."

Somewhat relieved, she finally noticed the evidence of the deflated bag hanging from the steering wheel. "It probably saved your life."

The man looked toward the front of his truck. "At least I'm better off than Blackie."

"Blackie. Who's Blackie?"

He did it then. He smiled. "Blackie is my truck." He started to climb down.

"Wait, you shouldn't move."

"I'm just going to stretch my legs and try to clear my head." He managed to get out of the truck and stood. She reached out to assist him, gripped his large forearms, then quickly released him when she realized he was doing better without her help.

"I think you should sit down." When he ignored her suggestion, she watched vigilantly for any sign that he might pass out. He seemed pale, but that could be the powder from the air bag. He didn't appear to have any visible bumps or bruises on his head, but she couldn't take any chances. "Do you want me to drive you to the doctor?"

He stared at her. "Why?"

"Because, you could be hurt and...I was the one who ran you off the road."

"You did kind of take your half out of the middle."

"I only glanced at my son, and when I turned back there you were. This is the main road to my ranch. No one comes this way, unless they have business at the Lazy S." She paused, knowing she caused the accident and couldn't afford to upset this man. "I know that's no excuse...." She brushed her hair from her face. "I'm sorry. I'm Dana Shayne. My ranch is the Lazy S and it's just over the rise."

He hesitated as he looked her over. "I'm Jared Trager."

She didn't recognize the name and she'd lived all her life outside San Angelo. No doubt he was a drifter. "Are you sure you're okay, Mr. Trager?"

He nodded. "It's Jared. I could use something for this headache."

"Then let me take you back to the house. You can also call for a tow truck from there."

"If it's not too much trouble."

"No, of course not," she said. She watched as he took a duffel bag from behind the seat then reached into the bed of the truck and took out a toolbox.

"You can leave that."

"Not on your life. These tools are my livelihood."

She'd known men who felt that way, but usually about their horses and saddles.

They started to walk across the road. At about six-two, with a sturdy build, Jared Trager didn't have any trouble carrying his belongings. When they reached her truck, he dropped his things in the bed then went around to the passenger side and climbed in. Dana hurried to her side and got in her seat.

"Mom, who is he?"

Dana twisted around toward her son. "This is Mr. Trager, Evan. Mr. Trager, this is my son, Evan."

Dana couldn't help but notice the close scrutiny the stranger was giving Evan. Then the man grinned.

"It's nice to meet you, Evan. Just call me Jared," he said as he reached back to shake the boy's hand.

Her son's eyes lit up. "Your truck got smashed up."

"Yeah, Blackie is a little banged up."

His eyes widened. "You call your truck…Blackie? I got to pick a name for my pony. Sammy."

"That's a good name."

"But I want a real horse. Mom says I'm too little. But when I'm six, I'll be big enough."

Jared Trager gave Evan the once-over. "I'd say by then you'll be about the right size for a horse. But your mom is the one who decides that."

Dana started the engine, before her son talked the man to death. "You didn't tell me why you're on this road."

He gave her a sideways glance. "I was coming to see you."

Jared wasn't prepared for this. He'd only arrived in San Angelo yesterday. After discovering the Shaynes and the Randells were conveniently neighbors, he'd asked around for directions to both ranches. Not sure yet if he was ready, if ever, to conquer the Randells, he'd decided to come to the Lazy S first.

More than likely this was how Marsh had first met Dana Shayne. Jared stole another look at her. Damn, she sure wasn't what he'd expected. Tall and willowy, she had a head full of wild auburn hair, green eyes that drew you in, while hinting at secrets. He had to admit that she'd taken him by surprise. Although pretty, Ms. Shayne didn't seem his brother's type. Hell, he didn't even know Marsh's type, or why he should care. He was here to fulfill a dying request, and that was all.

Jared blew out a tired breath. All the way from town he'd been rehearsing his speech to Ms. Shayne. How to relay Marsh's wishes for her and the boy. His strategy had been just to walk up to her door, say what he needed to say as he handed her the information about the boy's trust, then with a quick goodbye, he'd hit the road. What did he know about playing uncle? Family had never been his thing.

Now his plans had to change. How could he predict that Dana Shayne would run into him...literally? He gripped the edge of the torn bench seat as the truck bounced over a pothole. Hell, later he'd tell her who he was.

As they drove through the ranch's gate, Jared got a good look at the place. The Lazy S had obviously once been a showcase, but it had seen better days. The faded red barn and the once-white two-story house were both in need of paint. The corral fencing needed repair, as did the barn doors. He could spend weeks here and have plenty to keep him busy.

Wait, what was he thinking? He didn't need a job. He had one waiting for him in Nevada.

Dana drove up to the back door and turned off the engine. She climbed out and went to assist her son.

"You want to come see my pony?" the boy asked, his dark eyes wide. Jared hadn't missed the strong resemblance to Marsh. The same features and coloring. Surprisingly, finding this little version of his brother didn't make him sad.

"Not now, Evan," his mother said. "Mr. Trager's head hurts."

Jared noted the boy's disappointment. "Maybe later, son."

Dana and Evan led the way up the steps to the door. The wooden slats needed to be replaced, as did many of the boards in the porch. Inside, there was a mudroom with a washer and dryer and several pairs of boots lined against one wall. The temperature dropped when they entered a big peach-colored kitchen with floral curtains at the windows. An oval table surrounded by six chairs was the center focus, and on top, a big bowl of fruit. The place was so homey, it caused an ache in his gut for what he'd never had.

"You sure you're okay?" she asked.

He nodded as he leaned against the counter.

Looking unconvinced, Dana went to the phone on the wall and dialed a number. She walked into the other room and talked in muffled tones. In a few minutes she returned.

"Can I get you something cool to drink?" she asked.

"If you have some iced tea, that would be nice."

"I do." She went to the refrigerator where several pieces of artwork were on display. No doubt the boy's handiwork.

Evan pointed out one of the pictures, an abstract figure. "See, that's my pony. That's Sammy."

"He looks like a fine animal."

The boy nodded. "My grandpa got him for me for my birthday. I was three years old." He held up five chubby little fingers. "I'm almost five."

Jared frowned, finding he was curious about Dana's father. "Did he teach you to ride?"

Again the child nodded. "Then he got sick and went to live in heaven." He looked so sad. "I miss him."

Jared was happy the kid had been loved. "I bet you do."

Dana returned to the table with a glass of tea and one of lemonade. She handed the tea to Jared and set the lemonade on the table for her son. After the boy took a long drink, she said, "Evan, go change out of your good clothes."

"We're not going into town?" he asked. "What about my ice cream?"

"We'll go get some another time. We need to take care of Mr. Trager."

"Oh." That seemed to interest Evan more. "Is he gonna stay until he gets all better?"

"For a little while," his mother said. "Stop asking so many questions and go change."

"'Kay." Evan shot off, his footsteps sounding as he scurried down the hall and up the stairs.

"Sorry, my son is very inquisitive."

"He's not a bother," Jared assured her. Which was true. "Besides, I'm the one who's intruding on you."

"And I'm the one who ran you off the road."

He shrugged. "No one was hurt."

"Your truck didn't fare too well. And I'm not convinced you're completely all right. Your face is all red."

"It does itch. It's the air bag." He tried to make light of the situation. "I should have ducked to get out of the way."

She went to a drawer and took out a kitchen towel, wet it, then brought it to him. "Sit down."

When he did, she pressed the cooling cloth to his face.

He was taken aback by her casual manner. But it wasn't so casual for him. Her gentle touch definitely was causing a reaction.

"You could have been seriously hurt," she said.

"But I wasn't. So no need to worry." He took the cloth from her, but she didn't pull away. She was close. So close he breathed in her scent, a freshness he couldn't describe, but knew he could quickly become addicted to it. He raised his gaze to hers. Her eyes were a liquid green with tiny golden flecks in the center. His body began to heat up and he'd be lying if he told himself it had anything to do with the Texas weather. Finally he diverted his gaze.

She also pulled back. "I—I called Doc Turner anyway. He's going to stop by just to check you out."

Before Jared could argue that a doctor's visit wasn't necessary, he heard the door open and an older man walked into the kitchen. "Hey, you're back from the bank already? They give you the loan?" Just then the man noticed they weren't alone and his face reddened. "Sorry, Dana, I didn't know you had company."

"Bert, this is Jared Trager. Jared Trager, Bert Marley. We nearly collided on old Parker Road. I managed to get out of the way, but Jared's truck hit a tree."

Bert winced. "Well, jumpin' jackrabbits. Ain't that all we need. How bad?"

"His truck isn't drivable," Dana said. "But I'm more worried about Mr. Trager. The air bag went off."

Bert limped over and examined Jared through his wire-rimmed glasses. "Looks like you got a nasty rash."

"I heard that's one of the drawbacks," Jared said. "I was hoping I'd never find out, but I'll survive."

"Doc Turner's coming out," Dana said.

"What were you doin' out on our road?" Bert scrutinized him. "Take a wrong turn?"

Jared didn't miss the hostility in the man's eyes. This was the opening he needed. *But how do you just blurt out that you're the brother of the man who left you pregnant?* "No. I was headed this way."

"Why?"

Jared felt the beads of sweat on his forehead. "I wanted to talk with Ms. Shayne."

A grin spread across the old man's weathered face. "So you come about the job."

Jared was caught off guard by the question. He meant to say no, and tell the truth, but his answer didn't come out that way. "I guess I could use the work."

Later after supper, Dana went to her father's office. What a day it had been. She hadn't gotten to the bank to talk to Mr. Wilson about the mortgage. Instead, she ended up causing bodily injury to a stranger.

She was so grateful when Doc examined Jared and declared the man fit, then gave him cream for the rash. And by mealtime his headache was gone, too. All she had to do was send the drifter on his way. But something stopped her. Being a woman alone, she didn't like hiring somebody she didn't know. But thanks to her, the man was stranded. His truck would take nearly two weeks to repair so Trager couldn't leave for the time being. She knew that he might get work somewhere else, but she owed him.

It felt like she owed everyone, including the bank. Dana shook the worrisome thought from her head. Not tonight. Nighttime was for Evan. She walked into the living room and found Jared sitting in her father's chair with her son next to him as he read a story.

Dana's chest tightened. The picture of the two seemed so perfect. Father and son. But in an imperfect world, Dana knew she couldn't give Evan what he wanted the most. A father.

Jared raised his head and smiled at her.

Her son looked happy, too. "Jared was reading me a story, Mom. He's good, and he don't even have kids."

Jared shrugged, looking a little uncomfortable.

"I guess it's just a talent," Dana said. The man probably had many other talents. "I think it's time for you to go to bed, Evan."

Evan started to argue but looked at Jared, who nodded. To her surprise her son said, "'Kay, Mom." Then he climbed out of the big chair and came to her, giving her a hug and kiss.

Dana called to her son as he climbed the stairs. "I'll be up in a few minutes to say good-night." She then turned her attention back to Jared.

"I appreciate you spending time with Evan. He really misses his grandfather and…his father isn't in the picture." Why did she tell him all that? "About the job, if you're serious about working for me, you need to know I can't afford to pay you much." She quoted him the wages. "But I'll cook all your meals and you can stay in the bunkhouse."

"Are you saying you want to hire me? I'm not an experienced ranch hand. I'm a carpenter by trade, but I can ride pretty well and I've spent time on a ranch."

Dana hesitated, not needing any complications in her life…or her heart. But she had no choice. She did need a man. "That's what I'm saying."

He stood. "Thank you."

"Don't thank me just yet. Around here our day starts at five-thirty. Breakfast is at six-thirty and you'll be in the saddle by seven. And the day doesn't end until everything gets done. Think you can handle that, Mr. Trager?''

He reached out his hand and took hers. ''The name is Jared. And yes, I can handle it.''

Dana placed her hand into his callused one. Immediately she felt heat shoot up her arm, warming her entire body. Maybe he could handle the work but suddenly she had doubts about her ability to handle Jared Trager.

Chapter Two

He had to be crazy.

Jared tossed his duffel bag on the first bed in the bunkhouse. He'd had the perfect opening to tell her who he was, and he blew it. He puffed out a tired breath. Now what? He'd hang around a few days, help her out a little, make a few repairs. Maybe spend some time with the boy, then hand over the trust fund information and leave for Las Vegas.

"Damn." Pulling his cell phone from his pocket, he punched in Stan Burke's number. With the time difference, it was still early enough to catch him at the office.

The familiar voice came over the line. "Burke Construction."

"Stan, it's Jared."

"Hey, Jared. Where the hell are you?"

"I'm afraid I'm not in Nevada. And I won't be there for a while."

"What's the problem?"

"A couple of things," Jared began. "I need to do

some things for my brother and it's going to take a little longer than I expected. Especially since my new truck met up with a tree.''

''Are you okay?'' The sound of concern in Stan's voice touched Jared.

''Just a headache and a little air-bag rash. I'll be fine.''

There was a long pause. ''How long will you be there? We have a tight deadline on the Black Knight Casino.''

''A few weeks. I'll call a friend of mine—Nate Peterson. We've worked together before. He's a good guy and a top-notch carpenter. He can be there late tomorrow and help out until I get out of there.''

''Sounds good.''

''Thanks, Stan. I'll make it up to you when I get back.''

''All I want is my best carpenter back.''

Jared laughed. He'd been working for Burke Construction for the past three years. He liked Stan a lot. His friend was getting older and wanted to retire soon. Stan had offered to sell him the business. And Jared wanted to buy the profitable company. He'd have the money, but not until he'd receive his inheritance from his mother when he turned thirty-five or married. He doubted he'd ever marry, so that meant two more years of waiting.

''It's nice to know I'm missed.''

''Always,'' Stan said. ''Besides, you're going to help me reach those golden years of retirement.'' There was laughter, then a long pause. ''Is everything okay with you, Jared?''

No, everything wasn't okay, but Jared had never been one to share his problems. ''Yeah, just some family business. I need to be in Texas for a while.''

''Well, take the all time you need. Family is important.''

Too bad Jared didn't know who his family was. He gave Stan the phone number of the ranch. Next, Jared dialed Nate. Luckily the carpenter was in between jobs, and was excited about spending time in Vegas.

After a quick goodbye, Jared hung up and turned to find Dana standing in the doorway. She had on the same print skirt and white top as earlier. Her hair was down, curls brushed against her shoulders. She looked wholesome and sexy at the same time.

"Sorry to disturb you. I just came out to make up your bed." She walked inside, set sheets and blankets on the chair next to the single bunk, then began to make up the bed.

"You don't have to do that," he said. "I'm capable of making my bed."

When she didn't stop the task, Jared joined in. Accidentally their hands collided and Dana jerked back. Jared, too, felt the jolt, but continued to fit the pristine-white sheets and blanket over the lumpy mattress.

When finished, Dana glanced around the long room with five other empty bunks. "I think that's everything. I put towels in the bathroom down the hall." Her gaze shifted to his. "I'm sorry, but I couldn't help but overhear. Did you just turn down a job? I thought you came here for a job."

Jared froze. He could end this now if he told her the truth. *Tell her the truth, then you can leave.* "I couldn't make it to Nevada in time. Had a family emergency." He shrugged. "So I decided to stay in Texas for a few weeks. It's okay. I can catch another job when I get there. There's plenty of work in Las Vegas, especially in the construction business."

Dana seemed relieved. "It's not like that here. The small ranchers have been struggling for a while. I'm not going to lie to you. Most ranch hands want to work for the larger operations. They pay better.''

''You trying to get rid of me?''

''No. I need an extra hand now. I just wanted you to know that I can't pay the kind of money you're used to.''

''Let's not worry about that. I don't need much right now.'' He raised an eyebrow, wondering how she could manage with only Bert. ''How large is the Lazy S?''

''Ten sections now. Landwise I can handle more cattle, but we're in a drought and it costs a lot for feed. And I had to sell off quite a few head last year....''

''Sounds like it's been rough on you and Evan.''

''That's what it's like for most ranchers. Feast or famine.''

''Why stay in?''

Dana smiled and his heart tripped in his chest. ''Ranching is all I know, and the Lazy S is the only home I've ever known. I don't know if I could handle city life.'' Those green eyes rose to meet his. ''What about you?''

He hesitated. He hadn't been ready for her question. ''I've lived a lot a places over the last dozen years. Mostly large cities. Working in construction, I haven't spent much time in the country.''

''We move at a pretty slow pace here,'' she said. ''After Las Vegas, think you can handle it?''

At the moment Jared couldn't think of anywhere else he wanted to be. ''Yeah, I can handle it,'' he assured her. ''And I'm used to getting an early start. Like in Nevada. It's wise to start work before the sun gets too hot.''

Dana checked her watch. ''We both should be getting to bed....'' Color flamed in her cheeks. ''Well...I should leave and let you get some sleep.''

He nodded, trying to distract himself from the picture

she had alluded to. No, he couldn't think about her that way—about wanting her. "You're right. I'll see you in the morning. Good night."

"Good night." Dana turned around and Jared couldn't ignore the soft sway of her rounded hips. Desire shot through him. He knew the last thing he could do was get involved with Dana. She was off-limits, in more ways than one.

Jared sat on the bed, unlaced his work boots and pulled them off. Stretching out on the mattress, he stared up at the wooden slats in the ceiling. What had possessed him to take the job? He had no business being here. Well, what business he had wouldn't take more than an hour. He needed to forget what Marsh told him about their mother and just get the hell out of Dodge.

Reaching into his back pocket, he pulled out the crumpled letter from Jack Randell. Hell, why couldn't he just let it go? The last thing he wanted to do was find out he didn't fit in somewhere else. He doubted the three Randell brothers wanted a bastard brother showing up.

But, damn, he had to know where he belonged.

Dana walked through the back door of the house. She couldn't believe she had flirted with Jared Trager. And worse, she knew better. There was danger written all over the man, from his slow, easy saunter to his sexy grin. Besides, he had a home in Las Vegas. And probably a woman waiting for him.

As her father used to say, drifters come and go as fast as the seasons. If only she'd heeded those words when she'd met Marshall Hastings.

At twenty-three, Dana had had yet to experience love…until she'd met Marsh. A good-looking stranger who had come to the ranch, asking for directions. He gave her the attention she craved, but in the end he took off. Marsh hadn't cared that he'd taken her innocence. But he'd left her a gift. Evan. Because of her son she would never regret what had happened between them.

Now, at twenty-eight, Dana had given up on finding what her parents had. Although their time together had been short, Kathryn and Drew Shayne had truly loved each other. But their daughter would never risk her heart again. Dana never wanted to feel that kind of pain for the second time.

If she ever got married, she was definitely going to play it safe. Look for a nice, safe guy…like Hal Parks. The local deputy sheriff was nice enough, not bad-looking, either. She'd known him all her life. He still came around to the ranch and it was easy to see that, with some encouragement, the shy deputy might ask her out. Was that what she wanted?

Maybe. She had Evan to think about. He was getting older, and he needed a father figure. Hal liked kids, even coached Little League.

"If there were just a few sparks," she murmured, wishing she could get up some enthusiasm.

A warm shiver slid down her spine as her attention turned to her new ranch hand. Jared Trager sent off sparks with just a look from those bedroom eyes. What would his touch be like?

"Stop it," she chided herself, shutting off lights as she walked through the quiet house. On the stairs, not wanting to wake Evan, Dana skipped the fifth step to avoid the squeaky loose board.

Once in her bedroom, she closed the door and turned on the lamp on the night table. A soft glow illuminated the room she'd slept in all her life. It was still painted a light pink, but she had exchanged the twin bed for a double. After her father's death, she hadn't seen any reason to move into the master suite.

She went to the window and glanced down at the barn. Everything looked peaceful. Just the way she liked it. But for how long? How long could she hold on? How long would this ranch belong to a Shayne? The place was mortgaged and the payment was due soon.

A mortgage that her father had taken out when his only child had developed complications in her pregnancy and had delivered his grandson, Evan Andrew, six weeks early. At less than four pounds, her infant son had had to remain in the hospital for weeks. That had cost money, a lot of money.

When she'd told him of her pregnancy, not once had her father complained or lectured her. He'd never judged her when she said that her baby's father was not in the picture. And from the day she'd brought Evan home from the hospital, he'd loved the boy.

Now, it was just her and Evan. And as a legacy to her father and her son, she couldn't lose the Lazy S. She might not know what the future of the ranch would be, but she wasn't going to give up easily. She would do whatever it took.

The next morning, Dana was putting breakfast on the table when Bert walked in the back door, Jared behind him. His chambray shirt and jeans looked as if they'd already seen plenty of work and it was only 7:00 a.m. If Bert had had anything to do about it, they'd been up well before the sun.

"I hope you're hungry," Dana said as she tore her gaze away from her good-looking new employee. "Have a seat."

"Yeah, Mom made biscuits and her special gravy," Evan said from his chair at the kitchen table.

Bert hung his hat by the door. Jared also placed a hat on the hook next to the foreman's. She recognized the familiar battered straw that always hung in the barn. So her new ranch hand didn't even own a cowboy hat.

"Is it someone's birthday?" Bert asked as he walked to the table.

"I just felt like making biscuits and gravy," Dana replied, a little too quickly. "Of course, I'm not going to force you to eat them."

Bert grinned as he raised his arthritic hands in surrender. "Hey, I'm pleased as a calf in clover. Just surprised." The older man glanced at Jared. "This girl here is the best cook around these parts." He patted his rounded stomach. "I should know—been eating it for years. That alone should be enough pay to work here."

Dana returned to the table with a plate of eggs and a basket of her butter biscuits. "Yeah, too bad that isn't true. If it were, I'd have ranch hands lined up outside my door."

"Mom, I'll work for you," Evan volunteered as he reached for a biscuit.

She ruffled her son's dark head. "Thanks, but I'd be happy for you to pick up your room and give me a few kisses."

He puckered up and Dana leaned down and took his offering. "Bert and Jared need to give you a kiss, too."

Dana fought the heat flaming in her cheeks. She lost. "Oh, I'm pretty stingy with my kisses. I save them for my best guy. You." She tickled his ribs, making him giggle.

Jared sat back and watched the exchange between mother and son. Marsh would be happy to see how good they were together. Once again he reminded himself he should leave. It had been a lot of years since he'd worked on a ranch. Just that short time right after he'd left Graham Hastings's house some dozen years ago. He smiled to himself, recalling another time when he and Marsh were twelve and thirteen and attended a summer ranch camp for wannabe cowboys.

Maybe he'd just finish the week, then go and stay in town until his truck was repaired. While he was here he could replace some of the stall gates in the barn. How long could that take? He knew that Bert was limited to the amount of work he could do. Just feeding stock and keeping the fences repaired and upright was a full-time job.

That's what they'd been doing since five this morning when Bert had come to get him. Having had a restless night he'd already been awake. He'd been thinking about Dana, and the direction of his thoughts were dangerous. That's the reason he needed to finish this job and get going. His pretty boss was trouble.

"What ya doin'?" Evan asked.

Jared stopped his hammering and turned to find the boy standing behind him in the wide concrete aisle inside the barn.

"I'm fixing Sammy's stall. Some of the boards rotted out and I thought I'd replace them. You don't want your pony to get hurt, do you?"

The boy shook his head. "No, I love Sammy." He glanced around the barn. "Where's my pony?"

"I took him outside so the noise wouldn't scare him."

Evan gave the situation some thought. "Do you have a horse?"

"No, I don't."

"Do you want one?"

He pulled another rusted nail from the rotted wood. "I probably did when I was your age."

"Do you know how to ride?"

Jared bit back a smile at the artillery of questions. "Probably not as good as you, but I manage."

"I bet Mom will let you ride Scout. He's gentle and doesn't bite or kick."

"That's good to know in case, but I'm busy for a while repairing the stall." Jared replaced his hammer in his tool belt.

"Wow, what's that?"

"My tool belt." Jared crouched down to show the boy his different tools and the pouches for nails and screws.

"That's cool."

"I'm a carpenter. I need to have a lot of different tools so I can do my work."

"Can I help you? I know how to use a hammer. Bert showed me one time."

Jared scratched his head as if thinking about it. "I guess I could use a helper. Maybe you can hand me nails and tools."

The boy's dark eyes lit up. "Really?"

"As long as it's okay with your mother."

"She went into town. Bert's watchin' me."

"I guess we should ask him. Then maybe you can help me carry some more wood from the side of the barn."

"I'm strong, I can do it. Come on," Evan called as he took off to the corral to ask Bert. A smiling Jared walked after him as the boy eagerly chattered with the older man, selling his case. Bert looked toward him. Jared nodded his approval and the foreman gave the child permission. He found he was looking forward to spending time with Evan. He was a great kid.

The next two hours flew by. Surprisingly, Evan didn't get tired or complain about the work. The boy held tools, handed Jared nails and did just about anything Jared asked of him.

They were working on the third horse stall and Evan was still talking nonstop. The current subject was about some wild mustangs.

"Are there mustangs on the Lazy S?" Jared asked.

Evan shook his head. "They live in Mustang Valley, but that's really close to here." He pointed off to the west. "Over by the Circle B that Hank owns. He's Bert's friend. But Bert says Hank turned the ranch into a sissy dude ranch."

Jared couldn't help but laugh.

"They got a whole bunch of people who go there just to look at the mustangs. They pretend to be cowboys and cowgirls. Bert says it's plumb crazy. That city people are loco."

"How big is this place?"

"Real big." There was a pause as Jared hammered in another nail. Evan handed him another one. "They want Mom to sell them some of her land." The boy picked up the conversation. "But Mom never will 'cause when I'm growed up, the Lazy S is gonna be mine."

"So Hank has been after her to sell?"

Evan shook his head. "No. She says it's Hank's boys. They aren't really his boys, they just lived with him."

Was someone pressuring Dana into selling? "How do you know they aren't his kids?" Jared asked.

"'Cause Bert said they have a good-for-nothing daddy. Hank took them in and saved them from a life of crime."

"Who are these boys?"

"The Randells."

* * *

Dana finally had made it back into town. A lot of good it had done her. The bank hadn't been interested in listening to her idea to expand the cattle operation. Worse, they refused her the additional money she needed, only allowing her a sixty-day extension on her current mortgage. Things didn't look good. She turned off the highway and headed down the road to the Lazy S.

Why not just give up? She could sell part of the ranch to the Randells. Cade had talked with her several times about wanting the section that was attached to the valley and their property.

Dana wiped way her tears. She didn't want to think about it now. There was still an outside chance that she could scrape up enough money when she sold off her yearlings. But what would she and Evan live on for the next six months? She could get a job in San Angelo. But what was she qualified to do? Work as a waitress? And besides, Evan would only be in school half days. Bert would probably be able to watch him. But how could she ask her dear sweet godfather to do more?

She pulled the truck up to the back door, disappointed when Evan didn't come running to greet her. She climbed out and started for the barn, wondering what her son was up to. She was surprised to hear the sound of hammering greet her as she walked into the cool structure. She followed the noise and found her son…and Jared Trager.

The two had their dark heads together as they measured the piece of wood that was going to be a slat for the stall. Dana glanced around and discovered that several of the stalls had new boards and shiny new hinges. So this was what her new hand had been doing all day.

"Evan," she called.

The boy turned and grinned at her. "Mom, you're

home.'' He ran to her and hugged her. Dana relished having her son in her arms. It made her lousy day suddenly brighten.

Evan pulled back. ''Look what me and Jared are doing.''

She glanced around at the three stalls with the new wooden boards and gates. ''By the looks of things, you both have been busy.'' What was Evan doing in here?

Jared stood. ''I checked with Bert before I let Evan help me.''

The boy pointed to Jared. ''Look at Jared's tool belt, Mom. It's cool.''

Dana's gaze went to the area that had her son so fascinated. There were several kinds of tools that hung from a wide strip of honey-colored leather around Jared's narrow waist and hips. But her attention lowered to his fitted jeans over long muscular legs. A sudden awareness rushed through her body, catching her off guard with the sensual direction of her thoughts. Her gaze shot upward to catch a knowing look in the man's eyes.

''Yes it is,'' she agreed, a little perturbed that he'd discovered her bold appraisal. ''But you shouldn't have bothered Jared, honey. He has chores to do.''

''I finished everything Bert asked me to do,'' Jared assured her. ''I don't like to sit around. So I found a few things to fix.''

Dana stiffened. She didn't needed him pointing out that the Lazy S was badly in need of work.

''Evan, why don't you go to the truck and take the bag of groceries into the house?''

''But, Mom, I'm helping Jared.''

Before Dana could say anything, Jared spoke up. ''Remember what I said, Evan. You have to do your other chores before you can work for me.''

The child frowned, but he nodded. "Okay. But I'll be back." He shot out of the barn, leaving the two alone.

Dana watched him go, then turned back to Jared. "I'd appreciate it if you talked to me before recruiting my son. Besides, I hired you to feed the stock and repair the fences."

Jared stood there for a long time, then finally spoke. "I checked with Bert. He didn't have a problem with Evan helping me. I wouldn't let the boy get hurt. I only let him hand me some nails and help carry wood. I didn't mean any harm, Dana." He took a step closer and she fought the urge to back away. "What's really bothering you? If you don't want me around your son, just say so and I'll leave."

His gaze locked with hers and a warmth erupted in her stomach. She had overreacted. "It's not that. It's just…I can't afford to pay you any extra."

A smile spread across his face. "I don't believe I asked. As I said, I finished the jobs you assigned me, and thought I could fix a few things."

Dana blinked back threatening tears. She was acting silly. Was she jealous of this man because her son was drawn to him?

For so long, it had always been just her and Evan. He'd had a close relationship with his grandfather, but that was different. It wasn't a secret Evan wanted a father. And as his mother, Dana was terrified her son would get hurt attaching himself to every man who he met. In walked Jared Trager and he was getting the brunt of her wrath just because Evan longed to spend time with him.

"You're right. I apologize. I appreciate what you've done here." She brushed back her hair. "I guess I just had a bad day."

He cocked an eyebrow. "Any way I can help?"

She released a tired breath and shook her head. "This is something I have to handle on my own. The worst part is, it looks like there's only one answer."

Chapter Three

That evening, Jared walked toward the house for supper. Bert had gone up earlier and Jared had thought about skipping the meal and just staying in the bunkhouse. He figured if Dana hadn't wanted him around the boy, she surely wouldn't want him at her supper table.

It had been hours since she'd stopped by the barn and more or less told him to stay clear of her son. Normally, he'd never given a second thought to kids. But little Evan was starting to get to him. No doubt the boy was aching for a father. "He needed you, Marsh. You should have been here for him."

Emotions tightened Jared's throat and he stopped on the porch to pull himself together. Damn, he didn't want to do this. He didn't want to feel anything. Years ago he'd learned how to cover all the hurt his father dished out—he'd learned to turn off emotions. After he'd left home, he'd avoided any and all attachments. Whenever he'd hooked up with women, he told them up front not to expect anything permanent, nothing that would put him in danger of getting hurt. Now, he was smack-dab in the middle of this...mess. A fatherless boy who was his nephew. If that wasn't enough, about ten miles down the road, there was a whole other situation.

Jared looked off toward the west in the direction where supposedly the Randells lived. The last thing he wanted—or needed—was more family. He'd never fit into that cozy scene. An anxiousness rushed through him. This was usually when he'd pack up and move on. Too late. After turning up a hero to a little boy, and wanting to help out the pretty mother, he was already involved.

Besides, he owed Marsh this. He'd never been much of an older brother, so he had to stick it out. He could do this one last thing for probably the only person who had ever loved him.

"Jared?"

Jared recognized the child's voice and turned to see Evan coming out of the house.

He smiled at him. "Hi, Evan."

"Are you mad at me?"

Jared crouched down to the boy's level. "Of course I'm not mad at you. Why would you think that?"

"Mom wouldn't let me help you anymore. She said I had to clean my room."

"And that is what you needed to do. You should always mind your mother. Besides, I didn't do much more work on the stalls after you left. I had other chores to finish myself."

The boy's eyes rounded. "Did Mom get mad at you, too?"

"No. She's just worried that you might get hurt."

"She always gets afraid." He pouted. "I'm not a baby."

"Sorry, partner, that's just a fact of life. You never

stop being *her* baby. And it's only because she loves you
so much that she worries."

"But I'm gonna have a birthday. In July." He held up
his hand, his fingers spread wide. "I'll be five. I'm gonna
go to school, too."

"You are getting big. But we still have to listen to our
mothers."

"I bet you don't."

A sadness spread through him as he thought about the
fragile woman who'd stood in the shadows as Graham
Hastings ruled the family like he did his corporation.
Then one day Audrey Trager had gotten sick. She'd died
when Jared was only ten, taking so many secrets with
her. "No, but I'm a lot older than you."

Evan looked thoughtful. "You old enough to be a
dad?"

Dana stood at the screen door, shocked by her son's
question, and surprised to find Jared Trager there. She
had figured he'd be gone by now. Which was unrealistic
since he didn't have a vehicle to drive off in.

"I guess I'm old enough," Jared began. "I've just
never settled down and married."

"My mom isn't married. She's pretty and you
could—"

Hearing enough, Dana called out to her son. "Evan."

Both males turned in surprise.

"It's time for supper." She glanced quickly at Jared,
fighting to keep the heat from her cheeks. "You both
need to wash up." She headed back to the kitchen, knowing she had to have a long talk with her son. She didn't
want him trying to marry her off, especially to a drifter.

All through the meal, Jared felt invisible as the conversation centered around the next day's chores and Dana
directed her orders to Bert. Evan was quietly eating his

supper, obviously sensing his mother's sullen mood, and remained on his best behavior.

Smart boy.

Jared knew that he, too, better watch how far he went without checking with Dana. She wasn't a helpless female by any means. She had run the ranch and raised her child pretty much on her own. But something had happened today, something related to her trip into town that seemed to take away her fight. Did it have anything to do with her business at the bank? Bert had let it slip earlier that Dana was having trouble financing the ranch. Even Dana herself had admitted this past year had been a rough one.

Mind your own business, he told himself. Stay the two weeks as agreed, then just give Dana Marsh's letter and walk away. There was probably some money for her along with Evan's trust fund.

"Jared." Dana spoke his name, surprising him. "I want to thank you for repairing the stalls. I didn't get a chance to see everything, but Bert said you did a great job."

"You're welcome. I had a good helper." He winked at Evan.

"That's me, Mom." The boy puffed out his chest. "Can I help Jared tomorrow? There's lots of things broke."

Dana felt a sting of battered pride. Even though the condition of the ranch was evident to everyone, she hated to think even her son saw it, too. "I know, Evan, but you can't keep expecting to tag along after Jared. It's not his responsibility to—"

"The boy isn't a bother," Jared blurted out, then quickly took another bite of food.

Dana couldn't hide her irritation. "That's not what I

meant. I just don't want you to think that I expect you to repair everything around here.''

''Unless you have a problem with me replacing the wood in the stalls or corral, I don't mind doing it, and there is plenty of wood stacked behind the barn.''

''Yeah, Mom,'' Evan said. ''Jared's real good at fixin' stuff and Sammy likes his new gate. And I'm a good helper.''

Dana and Jared exchanged a look. Jared smiled, then said, ''Evan is the best helper I ever had.''

''See, Mom. Jared wants me to. Please…can we?''

Once again Dana looked at Jared. Big mistake. Those bedroom eyes were lethal. ''I guess it's not a problem if your other chores are done.''

''Oh, boy!'' Evan cheered, then jumped up from his chair and hugged his mother. ''I love you.''

Dana enjoyed the moment. Just as quickly her son released her and went back to his seat and began eating his least favorite vegetable, green beans. So there were miracles.

''Who wants dessert?'' Dana stood and picked her still-warm Dutch apple pie up off the counter.

Bert's eyes lit up. ''Hot diggity! Jared, you haven't lived until you've had a taste of Dana's apple pie. Won a blue ribbon at the fair four years in a row.''

''I guess I have to try it.'' Jared carried his and Bert's plates to the sink; Evan followed with his. Then Jared walked to the coffeemaker. ''Would anyone like a cup?''

''I wouldn't mind at all,'' Bert said, ''since you're up.''

He glanced at Dana. ''How about you?''

''Coffee would be nice.''

Dana turned back to her task of serving up dessert, allowing Jared to enjoy the view of how her jeans fit over her nicely curved bottom and long shapely legs. His body began to stir and he finally turned back to the counter and busied himself with the coffee.

"Jared, you want ice cream with your pie?"

He could only nod. Oh, yes, he definitely needed something to cool him off.

Around midnight, Dana couldn't sleep and, finally giving up, she made her way to the porch. So many times she would go sit on the old glider swing and enjoy the peaceful night. The sound of the crickets and faint scent of jasmine in the air was a quick cure to lull away the day's troubles. The ranch had always been her sanctuary. She loved it and wanted desperately to raise Evan here. But for the first time it appeared that might not be a possibility, and she had to face it.

Dana tucked her feet under her and tugged her robe tighter around her body. Where would she and Evan go? What would she do? Never in her life had she thought about doing anything else but ranching. She hadn't finished college. So what was she qualified to do to support herself and her child? There were so many things she had to think about.

She was desperate enough, she'd even thought about finding Evan's father, Marsh Hastings. The last thing she wanted was to drag a man into her son's life who didn't want to be there. Marsh had made his choice nearly six years ago. If he'd cared, he would have checked to see if something happened after their one night together. When he'd never called, that pretty much told Dana what he thought about her, and his child. A tear found its way down her cheek. It didn't bother her anymore, but for her son, it made her sad.

Evan needed a father.

A scuffing noise drew her attention and she looked up to see Jared walk by. "Sorry, I didn't mean to disturb you," he apologized as he stopped at the porch, then rested his foot on the bottom step.

The man had only to be around to unsettle her. "It's all right."

"Too warm to sleep?" he asked.

"And a little restless," she said. "I sometimes come out here when I can't sleep."

"I guess we're both plagued with the same problem. Walking sometimes helps clear my head." He stared out into the moonlit night. "It's pretty quiet here."

"Not like Las Vegas."

He shook his head. "Hard to tell day from night in that town." He was quiet for a while, then said, "I guess I better head back to the bunkhouse. The day starts pretty early around here."

A familiar loneliness erupted inside Dana as she watched Jared start to walk off. There had been so many nights when she'd lie awake, aching to share a conversation or a touch with another person.

"Jared?" She called out his name.

He turned around and looked up at her. When her throat suddenly felt sand dry, she swallowed. "You…got a minute?"

"Sure."

He took the three steps in one climb and swiftly he was standing in front of her, so big and intimidating. For a second she thought he was going to sit next to her; instead, he perched on the railing across from her. Still he was close, so close she could tell he'd taken a shower. She could smell a combination of soap and shaving cream.

"I wanted to apologize for earlier today," she finally said.

"It's forgotten."

"I had no right to snap at you like I did. I'm not used to people helping me."

"I was only working for my pay," he said. "I can understand about Evan. I shouldn't have let him get near tools without checking with you first. You barely know me...."

"I'm sure you were careful," she conceded. "It's just that...I know things are run-down.... Since my father took sick, it's been hard to keep up with everything." Darn, she didn't want to make excuses.

"So, you're going through a rough time. All of us have been there. I'm happy to help. If I have a little extra time, I hope you don't mind if I work on a few things around here. It's not a big deal."

"It's a big deal to my son." She had to make him understand. Jared Trager was the kind of man you didn't forget easily. "Evan is getting attached to you."

"I think he's a great kid, too."

She smiled. "Thank you," she said, trying to get the words out. "Soon you'll be moving on, and...I just don't want him hurt."

Jared studied her a while, then spoke. "Do you think that's wise, Dana?"

This was the first time he had spoken her name, at least, in that deep husky tone.

"You can't protect the boy from life," he went on.

She gritted her teeth. "I'm sure going to try. He's only four."

"He's nearly five," he offered. "And people have to say goodbye all the time. If I'm honest with Evan, he'll understand that I have to leave when my truck is fixed. Haven't there been other ranch hands that have left?''

Dana sighed. "Yeah, I guess you're right. It's just that since his grandfather died, there haven't been many men around...."

Jared knew he should get up right now and leave but something prevented him. Maybe it was seeing her with the moonlight dancing off her hair, or hearing the loneliness in her voice. Dressed in an old-fashioned white cotton gown and robe, her auburn hair hanging loose and wild, Dana Shayne resembled nothing like the bossy woman who'd hired him. Tonight she just looked vulnerable...and too damn tempting.

"What about you, Dana? Is there someone in your life?" He told himself that he wanted to know for Evan's sake.

She looked away. "No, not for a long time."

"Evan's father?"

She shook her head.

"He hurt you, so you're not going to allow another man in your life?"

Dana looked startled at his words. "As you can see, men aren't exactly pounding on my door."

That made them both smile. "Then the men in this town are crazy."

"No, they're smart. Not many guys want to raise another man's child, and take on a stubborn woman with a failing ranch."

Dana paused as if she'd said too much. "I think I should go inside."

She moved to stand up, when her foot caught in her robe and she began to fall forward. Jared's reaction was quick and he caught her. He grabbed her around the waist and helped her to stand.

Dressed in her thin layers of clothing, there was little left to the imagination. Dana's body was slim and lush all at the same time. Desire, like he'd never known, shot through him. It only grew worse when she raised her head and their eyes locked in a heated gaze. He told himself it was because he'd hadn't been with a woman in a while. Whatever the reason, he had to put a halt to it. He didn't need any entanglements, not with this woman. He released her and stepped back.

"I take it things didn't go well at the bank today," he said brusquely.

She tugged nervously at her robe, then brushed her hair back. "They don't think a woman can handle things on her own."

From what he'd seen, Dana Shayne was more capable than most men. He wanted to ask her how much she needed. "Can you survive?"

"Maybe. If I get a good price for my calves in September. But it'll be rough going for the next six months."

He hated to ask the next question. "Could you lose the ranch?"

She sighed. "There's a chance. There's one other thing I could do...."

"What?"

"I could sell a section of my land to the Randells."

Jared was tired of hearing about the Randells. They had haunted him since he'd read Marsh's letter and found out that there was a distinct possibility that Jack Randell could be his biological father.

A cold shiver went through him as he tightened the cinch against Scout's belly. The horse shifted restlessly as Jared checked the length of the stirrups. He hoped he hadn't forgotten anything. It had been a long time since he'd saddled a horse, but Bert had expressed confidence in him when the foreman asked him to ride out to check fence in the north pasture.

Jared took the reins and walked the horse out of the barn. Pushing his straw cowboy hat down on his head, Jared placed his foot in the stirrup, grabbed the horn and swung his leg over the horse. Surprisingly, it didn't feel that strange sitting in a saddle. He'd ridden horses during the brief time he'd done ranch work years ago, and luckily he remembered how.

Bert strolled up to him, wearing a big grin. "Lookin' like a natural up there."

"Hope I feel the same by the time I return. *If* I return."

"All you have to do is follow the fence line. Check for any sections that are down. There's a supply shack under a group of trees about a mile out. Can't miss it. You'll find everything you need inside. If you see Romeo, chase him back on the east side of the fence."

Jared shifted in the saddle, wondering how to make Romeo, the huge Brahma bull, do anything he didn't want to do. "You sure this is the best way?"

"This is a job you need to do on horseback. Besides, Dana took the truck. And you got the fancy little phone in your pocket if you get lost." Mischief danced in the old man's eyes. "If all else fails, wrap the reins around the horn and tell Scout to take you home." Bert then smacked the horse on the rump sending the horse and rider on their way.

Thirty minutes into the ride, the Texas sun got a little hot, but Jared enjoyed the easy motion of the horse. Following the fence line, he found a section that had been trampled down, but no sign of Romeo. He located the shed and materials. He spent the next two hours digging a new posthole, then stringing barbed wire. About noon, he took a break and sat under a tree, enjoying the shade and the two sandwiches that Dana had packed him. Drinking thirstily from the water jug, he stripped off his shirt and poured some water over his chest, hoping for a bit of relief.

Jared's thoughts turned to last night, and Dana. When he'd tried to sleep, her face kept reappearing in his head. He wanted to help her. But how? Making repairs wasn't going to stop the bank from foreclosing. She needed to find the money somewhere. Marsh. His brother had arranged child support for Evan's care. Jared made a mental note to call the lawyer. Could she use part of the trust money to help save the ranch? Or would Dana have to go to the Randells? And how much of the Lazy S did they want to buy? One would think it might be better to lose a small part of the ranch than all of it.

Jared released a long sigh into the hot still air. "Thank you, brother, for getting me tangled up in all this."

Deciding it was time to go back to work, Jared climbed to his feet. After putting away his tools, he climbed back on Scout and continued down the trail. After another mile the terrain began to change. Scout started down a steep slope toward a grove of trees and large shrubs. Under the ancient oaks, little sun filtered through the heavy branches, causing the temperature to be a good ten degrees cooler. It seemed like an oasis in the middle of a desert. Scout continued on toward a winding stream rushing over a colorful rock-lined bottom. The animal stopped and drank the cool water.

Jared dismounted and bent down to sample the inviting liquid himself. When he had his fill, he stood to see the horses. About fifty yards away a herd of ponies were grazing in the tall grass. Jared searched the area, realizing he might not be on Shayne property. Across the stream in the distance, he discovered the cabins dotting the landscape.

Mustang Valley. Was he in Mustang Valley?

He turned and continued to search the area. That's when he saw a man on horseback riding toward him. He was older, probably in his sixties. When he was close, he tipped his hat in greeting, then leaned his arm against the saddle horn. "You lost?"

"Could be. I'm Jared Trager, I work for the Lazy S. I was repairing a strip of fence. I think I might have wandered off course. I didn't mean to trespass."

"You didn't. You're still on Shayne land, but barely. Did that old coot Bert send you here to irritate me?" The man climbed down off his horse and walked up to Jared. He peeled off his cowboy hat, revealing thick white hair and friendly hazel eyes. "I'm Hank Barrett. This here is Mustang Valley."

Hank Barrett couldn't help but stare at the stranger. He knew two things right away. Jared Trager wasn't from around here, and he wasn't a ranch hand. But there was something about him that seemed familiar.

"Where you from, Trager?"

"Originally, Colorado, but now Las Vegas. I've been working there for the past three years."

"What ranch?"

"I didn't work for a ranch. I'm a carpenter by trade. I'm working for the Lazy S until my truck is repaired. I had a little accident a few days back and I need to stick around a while."

"I didn't realize that Dana had hired anyone."

"Does she check out everything with you?"

Hank cocked an eyebrow. Seemed like the boy was

mighty defensive. "No, but we look out for one another. Her daddy and I were friends."

"Is that why you want to buy her land?"

Hank was surprised. *So Dana had confided in this Trager fellow.*

"That you'll have to take up with my boys. I'm retired." He sighed. "I come out here often for a few hours to enjoy the peace and quiet."

"Would your boys be named Randell?"

Hank studied Trager again. He had brooding looks: black hair and deep-set eyes, reminding him of three others—Chance, Cade and Travis. "Could be."

"Would I be able to get in touch with them?"

"Depends. What do you need to talk to them about?"

"Jack Randell."

That evening, Jared drove his newly rented vehicle in the direction of the Circle B. After returning that afternoon to the ranch, he'd asked Bert to take him into town so he could get transportation. He came back with a Jeep Cherokee. He also could have used a brain transplant.

He was actually going to confront the Randells. Hank had invited him to the house to speak with Chance, Cade and Travis. His brothers. Half brothers, he should say.

He turned off the main highway, then continued down a gravel road. When he was under the sign that read Circle B Ranch, a large two-story house came into view. Further down were several outer buildings painted a pristine white all lined up next to one another and all surrounded by a lattice of fencing.

He pulled into the circular drive and turned off the engine. Hesitating to get out of the vehicle, Jared took the envelope from his pocket and looked it over once again.

So many feelings rushed through him. Everything would change when he shared the secret. He didn't have proof outside the letter, but he knew. He knew now why Graham Hastings had resented him all his life. Why he'd never fit in. He didn't expect to instantly find a family. Hell…he didn't know what he expected.

He puffed out a long breath and climbed out of the car. He walked up the front steps, but before he could ring the bell, the door opened and a tall brown-haired man appeared.

"I take you're Jared Trager," the unsmiling man said.

Jared nodded. "That's right. I came to talk to Chance, Cade and Travis Randell."

"Look, I don't know what you want, but if it concerns Jack Randell, it can't be good, so my brothers and I don't want any part of it."

A pretty blonde appeared. "Chance, where are your manners? Let the man come inside. Then maybe he'll tell us what he wants." She turned and greeted Jared with a smile. "Hello, I'm Joy Randell and this is my husband, Chance."

Jared shook her hand. "I'm Jared Trager."

"Come in, Mr. Trager," she said, and moved aside.

"Please, call me Jared." He followed her and stepped into a huge living room. A soft, inviting golden color covered the walls along with shelves of books. A pair of honey-leather sofas were arranged in front of a tall fireplace where two more men stood. No doubt Randells.

"These two other brooding guys are my brothers-in-law, Cade and Travis. Their wives, Abby and Josie, are in the kitchen making coffee. Would you like a cup?"

Jared shook his head. "No, thank you." He wasn't sure if he'd be staying that long.

"I'll leave you *gentlemen* alone to talk." She kissed

her husband's cheek. "Behave, Chance. Just listen to what Jared has to say before you throw him out."

Once she'd left, Chance spoke. "So, Trager, what do you want to talk to us about?"

Jared's throat dried up. "About two weeks ago, my brother died. He left me an old letter from our mother." He pulled the envelope out of his pocket and handed it to Chance. "It's from Jack Randell."

Chance opened the envelope and first pulled out the picture of Audrey and Jack. He studied it a while, passed it on to his brothers, then unfolded the one-page letter.

Jared could hear his heart pounding in his ears as an eternity seemed to pass. Finally, Chance handed the letter off to his brothers and looked at Jared.

"What the hell you trying to take from us?"

What did Jared expect? A loving hug and welcome to the family? "Not a damn thing."

Jared grabbed the letter and headed for the door. Once outside, he jumped into the Jeep and turned on the engine, then pressed down on the gas pedal and shot off, kicking up gravel along the way. He had trouble seeing the road as his anger, mixed with his emotions, nearly blinded him. Jared hated feeling this way. He gripped the wheel tighter. For years, he'd controlled the loneliness of always being an outsider, but tonight was the worst yet.

Back at the Lazy S, the Jeep skidded to a stop in front of the barn and Jared climbed out and slammed the door. He went straight to the bunkhouse and threw the letter on the bed. He wanted to hit something in the worst way—anything to burn off his anger and frustration. That was when he heard Dana's voice.

"Jared…" She spoke softly.

He looked up and saw her just inside the doorway. She was wearing a long skirt and pink blouse. Her hair was curled around her pretty face, her eyes were a brilliant green. From the first Dana had stirred something in him he didn't want to feel. He had to resist her. "This is not a good time." He worked to control his voice.

"You drove in here like the devil himself was after you." She came toward the bunk…toward him. "I don't know where you went or what happened tonight," she began, "and maybe it's none of my business…"

Hell, she didn't want to know what he was thinking right now, or what he wanted to do right now.

"That's right—it's none of your business."

Pain flashed across her face and it tore at his heart. "I think it's best if you leave, Dana."

She stood there for a long time, but started to turn, and that's when he broke and reached for her. Jared caught a whiff of her fragrance and was lost. He needed her— badly. When she didn't move away, he pulled her into his arms.

She looked surprised, excited, and came willingly.

"We're playing with fire," he breathed right before his mouth covered hers.

Jared didn't want to think right now. He'd save his regrets for tomorrow. All he wanted was the taste of her. To feel her body against his. When she opened her mouth, he delved deep to savor her sweetness, pushing all rational thoughts away.

Right now he needed what Dana Shayne could give him. For a little while, he wanted to pretend that someone cared for him.

Someone wanted him.

Chapter Four

Dana had never experienced anything like Jared's kiss.

His mouth was strong, but gentle against hers. Demanding and coaxing at the same time. She surrendered without resistance, opening willingly as his tongue swept inside like a thief. A hunger, like nothing she'd ever felt before, coursed through her. She moved in closer against him, aching for more. It had been so long since anyone had held her, kissed her...wanted her...

With a groan, his arms tightened around her, pressing her body against his evident desire. Her breasts tingled, begging for his touch and he didn't make her wait. When his hand moved under her blouse and covered her heated flesh, she was the one who whimpered. He pulled back and rained kisses down her jaw to her neck as his fingers teased her nipple.

"Oh, Jared," she breathed as she arched against his touch.

He raised his head to meet her gaze and a shiver went through her. Without a word, he took her mouth again.

The hunger only intensified and Dana didn't want to think, just feel. Those glorious hands of his found their way to her skirt. Cupping her bottom, he moved her against him, causing agonizing pleasure.

A sudden noise brought Jared back to reality. He pulled back and, ignoring the stunned look on Dana's face, moved to the other side of the room.

Soon the door opened and Bert poked his head inside. "Hey, Jared—" he called, then caught sight of Dana. The old man's gaze moved back and forth between them. "Dana, I didn't know you were out here."

Somewhat recovered, Jared turned around and looked at Dana. Mistake. Her face was flushed. She looked as if she'd been thoroughly kissed. He shifted his attention to Bert. The old man wasn't a fool. "Dana...just came by to tell me the schedule tomorrow."

Bert removed his hat and scratched his head. "Funny, I thought that was my job."

"Ah...Jared—" Dana spoke up "—just wanted to know if it was okay if Evan helps him tomorrow. I let him know that he doesn't have to feel responsible for my son." She headed for the door. "I'm going in. See you both at breakfast."

Jared wanted to follow her to explain what had just happened. But what the hell had happened between them? He glanced at Bert. The man looked as if he was expecting an explanation. Well, he wasn't going to get one. Jared took off after Dana.

There were patches of light on the way from the barn to the house. Jared saw Dana in the shadows just off the porch. He ran and caught up to her.

"Dana, I need to talk to you."

She stopped but didn't turn around. "I don't think there's anything to say."

"I think there's plenty," Jared insisted. "About what happened in the bunkhouse... It shouldn't have happened. I apologize."

"That's what every woman wants to hear—that a man is sorry he's kissed her."

Jared's frustration hadn't lessened. "That wasn't a kiss, that was an all-out assault."

Dana finally turned around. He could see the leftover desire in her beautiful eyes. "Was I complaining?"

He shook his head. "You deserve more, Dana. A lot more."

"Well, we don't always get what we deserve, do we?"

Damn. Marsh had really done a number on her. If she knew who he was, it would only make things worse. "I'm not someone you should depend on. I'm only around for a while. I have to get to Las Vegas."

He saw her fighting back tears. "Why don't we forget this night ever happened?"

Jared thought back to the scene at the Randells and wished the same thing. He knew it was going to be impossible on two counts, especially with what had happened in the bunkhouse. But if was what Dana wanted... He nodded. "Good night, Dana. I'll see you in the morning."

He watched as she walked up the steps. He wanted to follow her, to tell her everything, about Marsh, about the Randells. But he knew she would toss him off the Lazy S so fast. Funny thing was he didn't want to go. He wanted to hang around. She needed him. And surprisingly, he needed her...and Evan.

The next morning, Dana didn't have to worry about facing Jared. He hadn't come to breakfast. Bert said he had something to finish up before he rode out with him to the south pasture.

"Mom, can I be Jared's helper today?" Evan asked as he walked into the kitchen, dressed in his jeans and long-sleeve shirt to protect himself from the hot Texas sun.

Dana knew her son would push this issue as far as he could. "Honey, Jared has other things to do this morning."

"But you're the boss of him. You can tell him to work in the barn."

"I made Bert the boss and he needs Jared to help him. They're going to need to move some of the herd today."

"Can't they do that another day?"

"The cows and calves have to eat. And there's fresh grass in another pasture."

"So they get fat."

She nodded. "And we make more money at market."

"So…can I go ride with them?"

"Evan, we've talked about this. You have to wait until you're older." The boy looked dejected. He'd been alone for so long without anyone to play with. Hopefully when school started in the fall he would make friends.

If we still own the Lazy S, Dana thought.

"You know what?" Dana said. "Joy is coming by today and she's bringing Katie Rose with her."

Evan looked in pain. "But…Mom, she's a baby…and a girl."

Dana had to smile. She knew one day his distaste for girls would change. "I know she's only three and a half. But she likes you, a lot." Little Katie had toddled after Evan since the day she'd taken her first steps.

"She bothers me. She always wants to hug me, and she plays with dolls."

"Maybe today you can show her your Hot Wheels?"

"But, Mom," the boy complained. "I want to be with Jared. He needs me."

"Evan." A familiar man's voice drew their attention. Dana looked up to see the tall handsome man who'd suddenly turned into a cowboy. He had on a Western shirt, jeans and boots and all. He already had the long lanky build with all the muscles.

"Jared." Evan jumped down from the chair and ran to him. "Mom says I can't help you."

Jared crouched down. "Hey, buddy, I'm going to be pretty busy this morning. Maybe when I get back we can get in some work later."

Dana saw her son's eyes light up. "Can I, Mom?"

"If everything else gets done."

The boy's smile quickly faded as he looked back at Jared. "I have to play with a girl today."

Jared's jaw twitched. "Well, sometimes cowboys have to do things that aren't much fun. But remember, you always treat a lady with respect."

"What does respect mean?"

"That means you are nice to them."

The boy hung his head. "'Kay. I'll do it."

"And finish your chores without complaining."

He nodded. "'Kay, I will."

Jared stood up and ruffled Evan's hair. "Good. I'll see you when I get back." He looked at Dana. His dark blue eyes locked with hers, causing her body to warm. She couldn't stop the flood of memories. The feel of his hands, of his mouth...

She shook her head. "Did you need something else?"

He smiled. "I was just wondering if you had any left-over biscuits?"

"Maybe a few." Dana picked up the lunch sacks off the counter. Inside were two ham sandwiches apiece along with slices of peach pie and biscuits. "Here. This should keep you and Bert going for a few hours."

"Thanks," he said, then drew a breath as if he wanted to say more. But after a moment he turned and walked out the door.

Dana wanted to call him back, but nixed the idea. It was better to leave things alone. He was leaving in about a week. And she and Evan would be alone again.

Jared found he was getting comfortable with Scout. The buckskin was easy to ride. Even though the Texas heat had the temperature climbing into the nineties, it didn't bother him. Just Bert's sullenness. The older man wasn't about to come out and say what was on his mind. He could just ask Jared about last night. But no. He had to grunt all morning and refuse to talk. Well, that was fine. He didn't need to talk.

Hell, wait until Bert discovered that Jared could be a Randell.

They were nearly to the pasture and the foreman suggested they take a break next to the creek. They delved into the sandwiches hungrily and then Bert finally spoke. "Heard you drove over to the Circle B last night."

Surprised that the news got around so fast, Jared was caught off guard. Had Hank Barrett said something?

"Didn't know you had business with them," Bert said.

"I don't." Jared frowned. "I just had something they needed to see."

"So you're not doing business with them."

"No, I'm not."

"Good, because if you're here to try and get Dana to sell… That would upset her a lot." The old man's leathered face showed love and concern. "She talks tough, but when it comes to some things... She may have a child, but she hasn't had much experience...."

"You don't have to warn me off," Jared said. "I'm not planning on doing anything to hurt Dana."

"That's not what it looked like last night."

"What happened between us is our business, but if it matters to you, I've already apologized to her. It won't happen again."

"Good." Bert got up slowly, put his sack in his saddlebag and mounted his horse. "We better get back to work."

Jared gathered his things and followed Bert. Hell, the man was as grumpy as an old bear. But he was loyal to Dana and he obviously loved her and Evan. She needed someone to look after her. Jared just wasn't the man for the job.

He climbed onto Scout and tugged the reins toward the fence. They continued to ride about another mile until they found the downed fence. In the mass of tangled barbed wire there were two calves.

Two *dead* calves.

With orders from Bert, Jared was to move the bawling mama cows away from their babies. It wasn't as easy as it looked; the cows wouldn't leave the calves. With Bert's help, they managed to shoo them off, then Bert dragged the carcasses away as Jared started with the fence repair.

After about an hour, they were back on the horses. They had to round up the rest of the herd. That took a while. By late afternoon, they had the rest of the cows and calves accounted for and moved to the new pasture.

Now they only had to go back and tell Dana the bad news.

* * *

"I'm pregnant."

Dana gasped at Joy Randell's declaration.

She got up and hugged her friend. "Oh, Joy, I'm so happy for you. I bet Chance is over the moon."

The pretty blonde smiled. "He's been strutting around like one of his stallions for the past week." She sighed. "It's going to be a long seven months." Then she smiled. "I did make him promise that this time we'll make it to the hospital."

Dana was happy and jealous at the same time. Her friend had a loving husband and child, with another on the way. "You mean you don't want Chance delivering the baby in the barn this time?"

"Bite your tongue." Joy suddenly looked dreamy-eyed. "Of course that's one way to get familiar—real fast. When a man sees you at your worst, you know right away if he's willing to hang around. Maybe you should try it."

"Oh, once is enough. I'm plenty happy with just Evan."

"Are you? You don't get lonely?" her friend asked. "The right man can make all the difference. It did for Katie and me."

Dana couldn't deny that Joy was one of the lucky ones. She found a guy who loved and adored her. But memories of Marsh Hastings had made Dana bitter. "The wrong man can make a lot of trouble."

Just then the back door opened and Jared appeared. She had to bite back a gasp at his formidable presence. His shirt and jeans were covered with dust and mud as if he'd been wrestling a calf and lost. The day's growth of beard covering his square jaw only added to his appeal, as did his indigo-colored eyes and black hair.

Dana decided to act nonchalant, especially with her friend watching her. "Did everything go all right?"

Jared hesitated, then his gaze moved to Joy.

"So we meet again, Mr. Trager," Joy said, surprising Dana.

Jared nodded. "Mrs. Randell."

"I wish you could have stayed longer last night. I didn't get a chance to offer you some pie and coffee. And you probably could have used a little hospitality along with that."

"I got about what I expected," he said.

Jared turned back to Dana. "We found some fence down along with two calves who'd gotten tangled in the barbed wire. The calves didn't make it. Bert took care of them."

"Damn," she cursed under her breath. She needed anger to keep her from breaking down and bawling her eyes out. What else could happen?

"Sorry," Jared said.

She drew a calming breath. "It's not your fault. I knew those posts were rotted out. I should have replaced them weeks ago and this wouldn't have happened."

"They're replaced now."

"Good. Did you get the herd moved?"

"Yes. We took care of it. I need to get back and cool down Scout." He walked out.

"I'm sorry about the calves, Dana," Joy said. "I know how much you're depending on the sale...."

"Yeah, it's going to be close," Dana admitted. She couldn't afford to lose any—at all. "That's ranching. Chance, Cade and Travis were wise to branch out, to help with the lean years. How is the Mustang Valley Campground doing?" she asked, wanting to take the focus off her.

"With the lake stocked with fish, it's booked for the entire summer." Joy smiled, then her smile slowly faded.

"As much as I love the campground, it's a lot of work. And since I'm pregnant now, Chance is going to hire someone for the season." Her friend's eyes sparkled. "Dana, why don't you take the job?"

"I can't do that," Dana said. "I have the ranch to run."

"Oh, you have Bert to deal with the work here. If a problem comes up, you'll be close by. We already have a couple of college kids who work for us who could handle things. You can even bring Evan along with you. I know it's only until October, but the money is pretty good."

With the bank loan hanging over her head, Dana liked the idea of making extra money. "I don't think Bert can handle things on his own."

Joy smiled. "As if you hadn't noticed, you have a good-looking cowboy working for you." She leaned forward. "Tell me more about your Jared Trager."

Dana looked puzzled. "He's not *my* anything. Besides, I think you should be telling me. You seem to know more about him than I do."

"I don't know the entire story myself. Chance and his brothers are keeping quiet on this one. I only know it has something to do with Jack Randell." Joy looked at Dana. "And that can only mean one thing. Trouble."

That night after a long shower, Jared felt like a new man. Almost. It hadn't changed what was going on in his head. He knew he had to tell Dana the truth, and soon. How much longer could he go on like this? Not long. Not when she was so friendly with the Randells.

Jared walked out of the bunkhouse and took a stroll along the fence to eye his handiwork. With Evan's assistance, he'd managed to replace several boards in the corral. Maybe later on this week, he could get some paint on it. Yeah, right. He kept talking about doing things like he was staying here. He knew for a fact that any day, as soon as Dana Shayne discovered who he was, she would throw him off the property. Didn't matter that he was bringing her money for Evan. Even if it were a million dollars, she'd still toss him just on principle alone.

A cool breeze touched his face and Jared sighed as peace settled over him. He smiled. It probably had to do with the fact he'd been so busy working, he hadn't had time to think. A warning went off in his head. He was getting attached to this place. Over and over in the last few days, he'd fought those feelings for the Lazy S. He couldn't stay here.

Besides, the Randells didn't want him, and for sure, Dana wouldn't when she found out the truth. She was turned off of men, and Marsh's brother had to be the last man she'd want. He could leave and go into town and get a lawyer to do the job.

He turned to place his foot on the bottom rung of the fence and rested his arms on the top as he peered out into the dark night. He'd spent the afternoon with Evan as they worked on repairs. Dana was a good mother, but the kid was starved for male attention. And he was the boy's uncle. His blood. At the very least he wanted to stay around a while for Evan. Jared knew he wasn't father material, but he cared about the child. A few more days…maybe a week. What would it hurt to stay that long?

He started to head back to the bunkhouse when he looked toward the house and saw the flicker of the insect repellent candle on the porch. He heard the faint sound of the old swing creaking, then the outline of a small figure. Dana. As much as he told himself to keep walking, he knew he was going to stop. He was drawn to her. He had been since he'd arrived here. The kiss last night ignited so much more. Usually, whenever he found himself getting too involved, he was more than ready to take off. But here he was, ignoring all the warning signs and headed right into danger.

Jared stopped at the bottom step. "Looks like it's cooling down some."

"It will only help if we get rain." He heard her sigh. "We could really use it."

There was a long silence. Finally Jared spoke. "I'm sorry about the calves."

"It happens. I wish I'd been able to hire a hand sooner. Then I could have kept up with the work. It might have been prevented. I hate to think of those calves suffering."

Jake walked up the steps, then leaned against the porch post. "I can ride out again tomorrow and check the rest of the fences."

She shook her head. "You've already got the herd moved into a secure pasture—the section you repaired the other day. They should be fine."

"Will you be?" he asked. "I know you're depending on the sale from this herd. Can you make it?"

"I always get through." She looked at him. "I have a child— I have to. This is our home." Her voice broke. "We can't lose it."

Jared didn't want to think about Dana and Evan not living on the Lazy S. "Isn't that going to be difficult?"

She shrugged. "Why? Do you think I should sell to your friends the Randells?"

Jared was caught off guard by the question. "Who says they're my friends?"

"You drove over to their place last night."

How much should he tell her? "A long time ago, my mother knew Jack Randell."

She stared at him as if expecting him to say more.

"My mother died years ago, but I found an old letter...."

"How convenient, they're my neighbors." She raised those large green eyes to his and all he could think about was how she felt in his arms, the sweet taste of her mouth.

He shook away the thought. "There are things I can't talk about...yet, but believe me, Dana, I'm not trying to help the Randells get your ranch."

"That's a little hard to swallow when you show up here and then rush off to the Circle B. Chance, Cade and Travis have wanted a piece of my land for a long time. And you seem really interested in my business."

"If it's just a small piece of your land, why don't you sell it to them? No doubt the money would help you out."

He saw the anger flare in her eyes. "You know nothing about it. My grandfather worked hard to obtain this land—Shayne land. And it stays in the family. All of it. And before my father died, I promised him I'd never sell. So tell your friends the Randells no deal."

She stood and started to go inside when Jared grabbed her arm. "I'm not hooked up with the Randells. I'm just not ready to talk about my business yet. Now, you can believe me or not. Say the word and I'll pack up and leave right now."

"Don't threaten me, Trager. You show up here and get friendly with my son...and kiss me."

His grip tightened. "I like Evan—he's a nice kid. As for the kiss, okay, I overstepped on that. I already said I was sorry."

He saw her eyes flame. "And I told you a woman

doesn't want to hear a man say he's sorry for kissing her," she snapped.

His own anger rose. "Fine, so I'm not sorry. Hell, woman, do you want me to admit that I wanted to kiss you? That I want to kiss you again. Well, you got it. Hell, yes, I want to." He jerked her against him. "But all you have to do is tell me no, and I'll leave."

When Dana didn't move, Jared cupped her face. "Lady, you've been warned." His mouth covered hers. His hunger only grew when her mouth opened and his tongue swept inside. Her taste was a mixture of mint and coffee and it acted like an aphrodisiac. He felt his body tense and his need for her grew. He pulled her even closer against him and the kiss escalated, threatening his control and so much more. He didn't want to think about how deep he was in. He didn't want to think about things he couldn't have. Right now, with Dana in his arms, he felt he could have it all.

He finally broke off the kiss, then leaned down again and pressed his forehead against her. He forced a smile. "I promise you'll never hear me say I'm sorry again." He turned away and walked down the steps before he made her more promises he couldn't keep.

The next morning, Dana woke up with a smile. After her shower, she hurried downstairs to the quiet kitchen and saw the sunlight streaming through the windows. She shivered, knowing she'd be seeing Jared in a little while.

She hurried through her routine, making a stack of pancakes and frying a whole pound of bacon, knowing the extra could be used for sandwiches at lunch. She sipped her second cup of coffee while waiting for Bert and Jared to come in. They should be finished with their chores by now. She checked her watch, then heard the door. With her heart racing, she looked up to see Bert come in. Alone.

"Morning, Dana," he said, and went to wash up in the sink. Then he took a cup of coffee to the table. "You might as well dig in because Jared isn't coming up. He decided to finish some repairs in the barn. Said he'd eat some biscuits later."

"I didn't make biscuits this morning."

Bert grinned. "I can see that." He poured syrup over the stack of pancakes.

Evan walked into the kitchen and took his usual seat. "Where's Jared?" he asked.

"What is it with all the questions about Jared?" Bert said. "Can't a grown man decide if he wants to eat or not? Besides, he'll be gone in a few days."

Evan looked panicky. "Mom, I don't want Jared to go away."

She fixed her son a plate. "He's not going anywhere right now, Evan. But next week he has to go to Las Vegas. He has a job there."

"But we need him here," Evan said. "A whole bunch of stuff is broke."

"Evan, eat your breakfast. We'll talk about it later."

"No, Mom. Don't let Jared leave."

Her son had inherited too much Irish stubbornness. "Evan, you know Jared only planned to work here until his truck was fixed."

"But he can change his mind."

"Evan, we're not going to talk about this anymore. Eat your breakfast."

"I'm not hungry."

"Then go to your room."

The sullen child got up from the table and ran out of the room.

"What has gotten into that boy?" Bert asked, and shook his head. "Trager's a drifter."

Dana felt defensive for Jared. "That may be, but he's put in a lot of full days around here."

"You'll get no argument from me," the foreman said. "But some people just can't put down roots. Jared Trager is one of them."

Dana had heard enough. She picked up an empty plate and began filling it with food, then wrapped it up with a cloth napkin.

"So I get to eat by myself," Bert complained.

"If you're eating, you don't need company," Dana said as she headed to the door. "When you finish, I want you to check the windmill at the water pond in the north pasture today. I'd appreciate it if you'd hang around a few minutes until I got back." She didn't wait for an answer and hurried out the door. She headed to the bunkhouse, hoping to catch Jared there. She was tired of the man avoiding her. He acted as if she were trying to rope a husband. That was crazy. She'd dealt with one man who didn't want her, she didn't need another. Of course, she could get used to the way Jared Trager kissed. The way he made her feel.

Dana quickly stopped the direction of her thoughts. Jared wasn't going to stay. So she couldn't expect anything from him but a few heart-stopping kisses. The sooner she got used to that, the better. She was determined this time that she wasn't going to let another man hurt her.

When she arrived, the sleeping quarters were empty. She placed the plate of food on a table, so he'd have it when he came in. She started to leave when she saw Jared's personal belongs on the scarred dresser. There was a popular brand of deodorant, toothpaste and a brush placed all neat and orderly, except for an envelope sticking out of the black leather shaving kit.

Was this the letter Jared had talked about? She didn't mean to pry, but seeing the name in the corner of the envelope froze her. Marshall Hastings. Seeing the name of the man she'd once loved, Dana couldn't seem to catch her breath as her heart drummed away in her chest. How did Jared know Marsh? She pulled out the folded paper. The two hand-written pages started out with "Jared…" And ended with "Your brother, Marsh."

Dana collapsed into a chair.

Jared Trager was Marsh Hastings's brother.

Jared dried off his hands and walked through the doorway. The plate of food on the table caught him by surprise, then he saw Dana. She was sitting on a chair, looking upset. His gaze went to the letter in her hand and he realized his worst nightmare had come true.

"Let me explain," he said, knowing nothing would help ease the pain he saw on her face.

"The only thing I want to know is if this is true." She held up the letter. "Is Marsh Hastings your brother?"

"He *was* my brother. He died a few weeks back." He nodded at the letter. "As you already read."

"I know. And I'm sorry," she said, sounding sad. But that quickly changed. "Why didn't you tell me who you were?"

"I don't know," he confessed. "When I had the accident, I thought I'd wait. Then I saw the trouble you were having with the ranch and I wanted to help."

"Why would you want to help me?" Her voice was heavy with sarcasm.

"Because Evan is my nephew and…Marsh asked me to make sure he was doing okay. Why didn't you ever tell Marsh about Evan?"

She was fighting tears. "He didn't want to know. If he had, he would have called me...."

Jared could understand her anger. "That doesn't change the fact that I care about the boy."

"Well, you've seen Evan and he's fine. Now, pack up and get the hell off my property."

Chapter Five

Dana marched out of the barn with her head held high, praying she could make it into the house without breaking down. She'd almost made it when she saw the familiar Chevy Suburban coming up the road. The truck pulled into the drive and Chance Randell climbed out.

He was a tall, broad-shouldered, good-looking man. Funny, Dana had known Chance most of her life. He'd always been the quiet brooding type, until he met and fell in love with Joy Spencer. Now she never saw him without a smile.

"Chance. What brings you over here?"

"Hello, Dana. Thought we could talk."

"Tell me you're not here to hound me about selling the strip of valley land. Isn't breeding the best quarter horses in West Texas enough for you?"

He grinned. "I'll save that argument for another day. Besides, I have a wife and kids to support."

"I hear congratulations are in order. Joy told me about the baby."

If possible, his grin grew wider. "Yeah, it's pretty great. That's one reason I stopped by. Joy said you might be interested in taking over managing the campground."

Dana sighed. Her friend hadn't given her much time to think about the offer. "It was your wife's idea, but I can't. With only Bert to run the place, I'm needed here."

Chance frowned. "I thought you hired a hand. Trager."

"I did, but he's leaving. He was only working temporarily while his truck was being repaired."

He looked toward the barn. "Why don't you let me talk to him? Maybe I can convince him to stay a little longer."

"No," Dana said. "Jared has made up his mind. He needs to get back to Las Vegas."

"Would you mind if I speak to him about something else?"

Dana wanted to ask him about what, but it was none of her business. Jared Trager was not her concern anymore. "Sure, he should be in the bunkhouse." She started for the house. The last thing she wanted was to see Jared again.

Jared found he didn't want to leave the Lazy S. A sadness came over him as he said goodbye to Bert. The foreman was obviously confused over the turn of events, but didn't ask questions. Jared let Bert know where to reach him in town and gave him his cell phone number.

Angry for making a mess of everything, Jared knew that Dana wasn't going to be able to handle things on her own. But, dammit, she was too stubborn to let anyone help. There was nothing he could do; she'd kicked him out on his rear end.

Jared picked up his toolbox and walked out of the barn

where he found Chance Randell standing beside his Jeep. Great, this was all he needed.

"Look, I'm leaving so there's no need to run me off."

"I'm not here to chase you anywhere," Chance said, then glanced away. "In fact, I may have acted a little hasty the other night."

Jared went to the back of the Jeep and opened the hatch. He tossed in his bag, then his tools. "Doesn't matter. It was a mistake coming here. I don't know what I expected to find."

Chance pushed his hat back on his head. "Maybe a little friendlier greeting. We didn't exactly give you a Texas welcome. It's just that when our father's name is mentioned, it brings back some bad memories. The guy was a real piece of work. So you might not want to discover that he's your father, anyway."

"You're probably right." Jared started toward the driver's side door. He didn't want to deal with this. No more rejection today.

"If you're still interested in knowing the truth, I've arranged for a DNA test for you and me tomorrow morning at ten o'clock." He handed Jared a card with the lab's name and address. "Hope to see you there." Then he turned and walked off.

Jared stood quietly. Why would the Randells want to know if he was their father's bastard son? He shook his head and was opening the Jeep's door when he heard his name called out. Something tightened around his heart when he saw Evan running from the house. Damn. How was he going to say goodbye to the boy?

"Jared, don't go," the child cried. He was running so fast, he tripped and tumbled to the ground. He climbed to his feet and kept coming. Jared met him under a tree. "Don't leave," Evan cried again.

Jared caught the boy in his arms and for the first time in a long time wished he could call a place home.

"I have to, Evan. You know I have a job in Las Vegas."

The child swiped at his tears. "But I want you to stay here. Please. I'll be good."

Jared felt like a coldhearted bastard. "It's not you, Evan. Sometimes we can't do what we want." Jared looked up and noticed Dana heading toward them. "But that doesn't mean I'm going to forget you. We can write each other letters."

The boy sobbed into Jared's chest. "I don't know how to read or print very good."

"Okay, then I'll write you, and your mother can read the letters to you. And soon you'll learn how to write in school." He gripped Evan by his arms and made the boy look at him. "Now, I'll be going into town for a few days, but I promise I'll come by and see you again." He looked up to find that Dana was standing a few feet away. He could tell she wasn't happy about his plans. Too bad. He wasn't going to let the kid down. He knew how rotten that felt.

"Evan," Dana called to her son. "Why don't you go back into the house now?"

The boy glowered at his mother. "You're mean! Why are you making Jared leave?"

"Evan, that's no way to speak to your mother," Jared said, not surprised at the child's disappointment.

The boy hung his head. "Sorry…"

"Tell that to your mother."

Evan glanced at Dana and repeated the word. Then the boy shot off toward the house.

Jared didn't miss the hurt look on Dana's face. "Don't take it so hard. He'll forget about me soon."

"If you hadn't come here…"

"Look, I know I messed up," he began. "I should have told you about the trust Marsh set up for Evan." Jared went to the back of the Jeep, took out a folder from his bag and handed it to her. "I should have delivered this that first day. Inside, there's the name of the lawyer you should contact."

"Thanks," Dana said, and pulled a small piece of paper from her pocket. "Here's the wages I owe you for two weeks' work."

Jared shook his head. "No, I don't want your money."

Dana's chin came up. "I don't take charity, Jared." She pushed the check at him.

Angry, Jared snatched the piece of paper from her fingers, then proceeded to tear it up. "Think of it as a gift for Evan. After all, he is my nephew."

"Too bad you couldn't be honest about that."

"I'm sorry for that, too. But don't punish the boy for my mistake. Let me write to him."

"I don't know if that's such a good idea."

"Like it wasn't a good idea to tell him about his father," Jared accused.

"Evan's too young to understand."

"Then why has he been asking me so many questions?" He stepped closer and he saw Dana's eyes widen. He inhaled her intoxicating scent, reminding him of the kisses they'd shared. His body sprang to life and he quickly backed away. "At least don't lie to him, Dana. He'll come to hate you for it. Evan deserves to know the truth about Marsh, if not now, then sometime soon. If only to help him understand who he is."

Jared turned and walked to the vehicle, wishing with all his heart that he could stay.

*   *   *

After Jared got a motel room in San Angelo, he called the body shop to check the progress on his truck. The manager said the repairs would take a few more days. Great. He was stuck in town. Since he had to stay anyway, he might as well go through with the DNA test tomorrow. He'd come all this way to Texas, why not find out for sure if he was a Hastings or a Randell? Even if, in his heart, he knew the truth.

When Jared phoned Chance to tell him he'd be at the lab in the morning, he was surprised to get an invitation to come out to his ranch. Jared thought about not accepting, but curiosity got the best of him. Besides, what else did he have to do but sit around the motel room, or hang out at one of the local bars and think about Dana Shayne?

Jared followed Chance's directions to the Randell Family Horse Ranch. He turned off the highway onto the gravel road that led him through a wrought-iron archway, then to a big two-story, yellow-and-white Victorian house. The lawn, despite the drought, was a rich green with colorful flowers edging the large wraparound porch and brick walkway. Two big dogs, a chocolate and a blond Lab came running toward him, then stopped and sat down at his feet, waiting to be petted. Finishing the playful exchange with the dogs, he looked up as Joy Randell and a little girl walked out onto the porch.

She greeted him as he came up the walk. "Hello, Jared. This is our daughter, Katie."

The small child with light blond curls turned shyly and buried her head in her mother's skirt as he came closer.

"Hi, Katie," he said. "I know a friend of yours. Evan."

The girl's eyes sparkled as she looked up at him. "Eban plays with Katie. And I play with his cars."

Jared smiled. "And I bet that's fun." He turned his attention to Joy. "Thank you for inviting me."

She smiled, too. "You're welcome."

He stepped up on what was obviously a new porch floor. The tongue-and-groove oak had been left natural, with only a high gloss polyurethane coating used to protect the finish. It was a first-class job. Most of the railing had been replaced and painted a snowy white to match the house trim. Several plants hung from above, adding color to the inviting porch.

"You have a beautiful home, Mrs. Randell."

She laughed. "You should have seen it when I inherited it. Made Dana's place look like a showcase. Chance did a lot of the work himself. And please, call me Joy."

"Well, Joy, he knew what he was doing."

"That's right, you're a carpenter by trade."

He nodded as he examined the structure. "I normally work on new construction, but it's got to be satisfying to restore a place like this."

"I'm glad we took the time. And believe me, it's taken nearly three years to get to this point. There's still so much to do. It would be nice if Chance had help." Those big blue eyes lit up. "You wouldn't want to do some side work, would you?"

"I'm not staying that long."

"Oh, I thought..." She smiled again. "You know, Chance is in the mare's barn. If you want, you can go down there. I'm sure he'd love to show you around."

"I'd like that." Jared followed Joy's direction to the new white barn. It was cool inside and quiet, except for the sound of a deep baritone voice. Curious, Jared followed the soft, almost seductive tone to a stall where he found Chance talking sweetly to a very pregnant mare.

He was surprised at the gentleness the big man showed

to the animal. Chance's love for this horse was evident in his voice and touch. "Does your wife know you talk to other women like this?"

Chance continued to stroke the mare's oversize stomach. "She doesn't care as long as the foal this lady produces comes out healthy and maybe even is worth some money." He glanced up. "Jared, meet Glory Girl."

Jared stepped closer to the railing and rubbed the horse's face. The chestnut with the white star on her forehead was a beauty. And friendly. She nuzzled closer.

"Well, hello beautiful," he crooned as Chance looked on. "When is she due?"

"Sometime next week. She's delivering late in the season, but her foals are well worth it." He came out of the stall and closed the gate behind him. They started to walk away and the mare let him know her irritation with a loud whinny.

Jared looked around the structure. All the stalls were freshly painted and clean. Several horses came to their gates, wanting attention.

"This is quite a place here," Jared said. "How many horses do you have?"

"Ten that I own. And another dozen that are in different stages of training. I'm alone right now, but I have two trainers and three groomers who work during the day."

"Impressive."

"It's a lot of work, too," Chance admitted. "Especially now since our expansion with the guest ranch and campground. Joy's pregnant, too."

"Congratulations." It seemed to Jared that the man had everything.

Chance smiled as he puffed out his chest. "We're both pretty happy about it."

Jared couldn't figure Chance out. Why would he care about finding out if they were related?

He looked at Jared. "Thanks for coming tonight. I have to apologize again for my behavior when you came by Hank's the other evening. After I talked it over with Cade and Travis, we all decided we'd like to find out if you're kin to us. Besides, you had no control over who your parents were, any more than we did. Believe me, Jack Randell is no prize."

"Do you have any idea where he is now?"

Chance shook his head. "Nor do I want to know. The last time Jack contacted any of us was about ten years ago when he got out of prison. He wanted money. I said no, and we never heard from him again." He shrugged. "It doesn't matter. As far as my brothers and I are concerned, Hank is our father. He was the one who raised us." Chance made a snorting sound. "Jack was just the sperm donor. Hank always said, you don't have to be blood to be family."

Jared knew Graham Hastings hadn't believed that. The man despised him. "Look, I want you to know that if it turns out that we're related…I don't want anything. I just need to know who I am."

Chance drew a breath and released it slowly. "That's good, because around here, we earn our place. I do have a concern, though. Dana Shayne. I don't want her hurt. Are you planning to hang around?"

Jared didn't like the third degree, but he understood it. "I have a job in Las Vegas, but I also have a commitment to my dead brother. Evan is my nephew." That was all Jared said, knowing any more of the story would have to come from her.

Chance shook his head. "I'm surprised Dana didn't run you off with a shotgun." The tone of his voice turned threatening. "I'll do worse if I find out you hurt her or her boy."

"I haven't done anything but try to help her. I know now it was wrong not to be honest with her when I first arrived, but it's not an easy thing to bring up in conversation. But Evan is my nephew and I want to make sure everything is okay with him. Since I discovered the trouble Dana is having keeping the ranch, I feel I need to hang around to make sure she and Evan will be all right."

"Dana won't like that," Chance admitted. "We've tried to help her many times. Sure, we'd like to have the land along Mustang Valley, but not to buy her out completely. She can't run the place on her own. And Bert... He's too old to handle much more."

"If the bank takes it over, where would she go? What would she do?"

Chance shrugged. "Joy asked Dana to take over managing the campground for the summer, but it's not enough to pay off the balloon payment that's due."

Jared didn't want to think about Dana and Evan losing the ranch. The Lazy S was their home. All the money in Evan's trust was tied up tightly, specifying it was only to be used for the boy's support and education.

Jared had the money in his trust, but he couldn't claim it until he was thirty-five...or married.

"What if Dana had a partner? Could she make a go of it if she increased the size of her herd and had a few more ranch hands to help run the place? Could she make a decent living?"

"That's a question I can't answer. Several ranchers have lost out, but then others have found ways to make it work. I breed and train horses. The Randells have also gone into the tourist business. Nothing is impossible if you're willing to work at it. Why? You planning to go into cattle ranching?''

"It's a possibility. A good possibility.''

Chance laughed, then sobered. "You're serious.''

"Just don't say anything to Dana yet. I think I may have a way to help her, but I need to make some calls. If it all works out, then Dana can have her dream and Evan can have his legacy.''

The next morning, Jared accomplished a lot. He called his lawyer, went to the bank and had a DNA blood test, all before noon.

Right now he needed to talk to Dana. They had to discuss the future before he could move forward. He pulled up in the driveway and got out of the Jeep just as Dana walked out the back door. His heart jolted at the sight of her dressed in snug-fitting jeans and a white blouse that showed off her perfect curves. Her copper hair was pulled back and braided down her back.

She came toward him. "What do you want, Trager?''

"I need to talk to you, Dana.''

"We said everything we needed to say.'' She began to walk away.

"I think you need to listen to what I have to say. It's about the ranch.''

She swung around. "What could we possibly have to discuss…and about *my* ranch?''

"I want to help you save the Lazy S.''

"I can do that without you.''

"You can't make the payment that's due in six weeks.''

Her eyes narrowed. "How did you know about that?''

"It wasn't hard to find out.''

"Get off my land.''

"Not until you listen to me. I want to help. You can't lose everything just because of your dislike for me. Think about Evan. I want him to have the Lazy S, too. Just give me ten minutes to explain."

She glared at him. "Why should I? You've done nothing but lie since you've come here."

"Because what I have to say just might save your and Evan's home."

"You've got ten minutes. That's it." She turned and marched up the steps and he followed.

Inside, she took him into the office, a dark paneled room with worn carpet that hadn't been replaced in years. Dana sat behind the desk. "All right, the clock has started."

No pressure at all, he thought. "It's no secret that you've had a few bad years because of the drought and you've had to sell off a lot of your herd before it was time. Now you're behind in your payments to the bank and the balloon is coming due. And the sale from your remaining herd isn't going to be enough." He studied her for a moment. "I have a solution for both of us."

Dana stared at him. "Well, don't stop now just when it's getting interesting."

"I've also talked to Mr. Janny, the lawyer in charge of Evan's trust fund. Although the fund Marsh set up is a considerable amount, Evan won't receive the bulk of the money until he's twenty-one. There will be monthly checks coming to you for his support, but Mr. Janny isn't going to give you any money toward the ranch."

"I couldn't use any of Evan's money. I want him to have that for college."

Jared nodded. "Not even to save the Lazy S for him to inherit one day?"

She swallowed hard. "That's a big risk. If I lose it,

then he'll end up with nothing. At least if I sell the Mustang Valley section to the Randells, I can keep part of the ranch.''

"What if I told you that I have the money you need? That I want to be your partner?''

"You've got to be crazy. Why would you want to get into the cattle business?''

"Because Evan is my nephew and I want to make sure he's taken care of.'' And because he hated seeing the pain in Dana's eyes. "I have money from a trust fund of my own.''

"And you want to give me some of it.'' She shook her head as if she didn't believe any of it. "What's in this for you?''

He hesitated. This was the tricky part. "The trust is sizable. I had planned to use part of the money to buy the construction company where I work in Las Vegas. But there is a stipulation in the will...and that's where I need your help.''

She frowned. "Need me? For what?''

"To marry me.''

Chapter Six

"Marry you!" Dana said, unable to believe his insane suggestion. "You can't be serious."

"I'm serious all right. You're in deep financial trouble. Unless you sell some of the ranch to the Randells, you're not going to make the bank payment that's coming due."

She straightened. "I'm not selling any of my land." She hated him knowing her business. "There's some time left."

"Time for a miracle?"

She'd been praying for one. Surely this wasn't it. "I'm not desperate enough to marry you," she said, then wished she could take back the stinging words.

"You better get desperate real fast, because you're running out of time...and you could lose the ranch because of your stubbornness." He started out of the room.

Dana hurried from around the desk. "I'm not being stubborn," she insisted. "I'm cautious." When he turned and stared at her with those hard sapphire eyes, her heart skipped a beat. Jared Trager made her crazy. "Why are you doing this?"

"Hell if I know." He looked confused and frustrated as he ran his fingers through his hair. "For Evan. That's why I'm doing it. I want him to be able to grow up here—in his home. On this ranch. He's already gotten a raw deal from Marsh."

Jared paused, seeming surprised at what he told her. He began to pace. "I'm also doing it so I don't have to wait until I'm thirty-five, roughly two more years to collect my inheritance and get my dream. To buy Burke Construction. Stan Burke wants to retire soon. He's been allowing me to buy into the business little by little. But if I had my inheritance now I could take over and purchase new equipment for the company." His gaze met hers. "You told me you could make a go of the ranch if you enlarged the herd. To do that you need money to hire more help and make some needed repairs."

"Do you know how much that's going to cost?"

"I have an idea, and I have the money to do it." He folded his arms across his chest. "Dana, Evan needs you to be his mother. You can't work twelve-fourteen hours a day and be his only parent, too."

"Are you saying that I'm not a good mother?"

"No, you're a great mother. You can have that dream—we both can have our dream, but we need each other."

"Surely there's someone else in your life that you could ask to marry you?"

He glanced away. "I'm not good at relationships. I'm doing this mainly for Evan's sake."

Dana couldn't believe it. She was actually considering his crazy scheme. The offer was so tempting. And it could be her only chance to turn the Lazy S into a successful ranch. "My dream is bigger than just raising cattle, Jared. I'd also like to breed some good saddle horses, and have a boarding stable."

So Dana was interested. Jared didn't know if he should be happy or not. "All that's a possibility."

She folded her arms across her chest. "If we decided to get married…how soon do you think—"

"As soon as possible. I don't receive the money until I have a marriage certificate."

"Of course it wouldn't be a real marriage." She gave him a questioning look. "I mean, you can't expect me— us…"

He bit back a groan. Oh, he wanted her all right, and if she were honest she'd admit she wanted him, too. The two times they'd been together diminished any doubt of that. They'd been nothing less than explosive. "To consummate the marriage," he finished for her.

She nodded as a blush colored her cheeks.

"If you're worried I'm going to jump you, I'm not. And if you want to take our relationship any further, that's up to you."

Dana released a breath. "No, that wouldn't be wise. So we're agreed that we're business partners."

"I want to have some say, but mostly I'll be a silent partner."

Her gaze met his. "I won't sign away any part of the ranch to you."

"I don't expect you to, nor do I want your land. I only want to look out for Evan's interest. He's my big concern."

"And you'll be willing to invest in the ranch with only a signed note? With no claim on the Lazy S?"

"No claim. I have no doubt that you'll do everything in your power to keep the Lazy S for your son," he said.

She started to speak and he stopped her.

"Dana, before you decide, there's something you should know. I came to San Angelo for another reason, too. It was the same reason that brought Marsh over here five years ago. He'd found an old letter that was addressed to our mother from Jack Randell. Seems they knew each other years ago. It also seems there's a chance that I could be Jack's son. I've taken a DNA test along with Chance and the results should be back soon. The outcome doesn't have anything to do with my offer—I just thought you should know."

Dana was trying to hide her shock. Jared Trager could be a Randell. She could see some resemblance, the similar build and square jaw. Those deep-set eyes were the most telling, at the same time they held so much back. "Thank you for being honest about that."

"So it's all right that we go ahead?"

She hesitated. "I have another question. How long will this marriage last?"

He shrugged. "I don't think my mother's will stipulates any time constraints. Why? Is there someone in your life?"

"No. Is there someone in yours? I mean in Las Vegas." Surely there wasn't, not with the way he'd kissed her.

"No one. But I can't stay in Texas indefinitely. Two or three months to get things going here is what I planned on. Then I need to get back to Vegas."

She suddenly realized how her son would be affected. "Oh, what about Evan? He's going to get attached to you."

"He's attached to me now."

That was the truth. Her son had barely spoken to her

since she'd sent Jared away. "I know, but it will get worse."

"Dana, I plan to stay in touch with Evan no matter what you decide about us." He took a step closer to her. He was a big man and towered over her, but she didn't feel intimidated by his size. "He's my nephew and I want to be there for him. I never had that with my father...." His voice drifted off, then his gaze met hers. "I want him to know that he can count on me."

What about her? Dana wondered. What was going to happen to her when Jared left her with a broken heart? Somehow she had to make sure she kept everything impersonal.

"If you need more time..." he began.

"No. I only need to make sure that you agree to keep this...situation strictly business. Our arrangement isn't going to be more than a marriage in name only."

"If that's what you want," he said. "I can stay in the bunkhouse."

She shook her head. "No. You can move into a bedroom upstairs. There's going to be enough questions as it is."

"Then you agree?" he asked again.

Dana drew a long breath and released it. "Agreed."

"I'll call my lawyer and let him know that there's going to be a wedding. As soon as I send him a copy of the marriage certificate my inheritance will be transferred into my account. Then I'll take care of the mortgage."

She gasped. "I can't let you pay the mortgage off."

"Might as well start with a clean slate." He quickly changed the subject. "So, you want to do this in a church, or at the courthouse?"

How could he act so nonchalant about it? Because it didn't mean anything more to him than a business deal.

That's how she needed to handle it, too. This was a way to keep the Lazy S for her son. It was the only reason for agreeing to this crazy idea.

"I think the courthouse. But I have one other request. I don't want people to know the real reason we're getting married."

Jared leaned toward her, and his gaze darkened. For a moment, Dana thought he was going to kiss her. "I doubt I'll have any problem convincing people that you and I are truly married."

Two weeks later, Dana was still trying to talk herself out of this so-called marriage. As Joy helped her get ready at the courthouse, Dana was fighting with herself not to call the whole thing off.

Surprisingly, Bert hadn't tried to talk her out of this marriage. And forget Evan. He'd wanted a dad for so long, he'd been crazy about the idea of Jared taking the position. In keeping with their promise, Dana had only told one person, Joy, the real reason she and Jared were getting married today. Even after signing the legal papers to protect her and Evan from Jared making any claim on the ranch when the marriage ended, Dana knew that there was nothing to protect her heart.

Now more doubts rushed through her head. "Am I crazy, Joy?"

Her friend sat beside her on the bench. "Do you hate Jared?"

"Of course not."

"Do you think that he's being honest about wanting to help you?"

"Yes."

"Could you fall in love with him?"

Dana thought back over the past weeks. Jared had

worked tirelessly, then spent extra time doing needed repairs. He'd been nothing but kind and thoughtful to Evan. What was there not to love? "Yes," she admitted. "That's what I'm afraid of."

Her friend smiled. "I know the feeling. I felt the same way about Chance. I was scared about marrying him, too. I had a baby and I needed him so much." Joy's sympathetic gaze met Dana's. "I think Jared needs you just as much. Men try to act tough, but they need love, too. I've gotten to know Jared a little better in the last week. He's quiet and distant sometimes as if he doesn't quite know where he fits in. He needs you and Evan. He needs a family."

"He has Chance, Cade and Travis. They're his family."

"Jared needs you, too, Dana."

"I'm afraid to let myself get close. He's going to leave and go back to Las Vegas."

"Then figure out a way to make him want to stay."

"I don't know how." She brushed away a tear. "The only man I've ever cared about was Marsh."

Joy patted her hand. "There's more room in your heart believe me. I felt the same way about Blake, and when he died, I never thought there would be anyone else. Then I met Chance. Just give yourself a little time. If it's meant to be, it will happen." With an understanding smile, she stood up and pulled Dana with her. "Come on, we have a wedding to get started."

Dana brushed imaginary wrinkles from the peach-colored dress Joy had loaned her. A soft sheer layered skirt hung to a princess length, making her feel feminine. The simple fitted bodice emphasized her small waist, and the neckline dipped low, exposing more cleavage than Dana ever dared before. Around her neck she wore her grandmother's cameo necklace. Her hair had been pinned up and baby's breath adorned the crown of her head.

"How do I look?"

Joy smiled. "The expression on your soon-to-be husband's face says it all."

Dana turned around and saw Jared standing across the room next to Chance. Although the DNA test hadn't come back yet, there was no doubt in her mind they were related. Tall, dark and so handsome. Jared had on a navy suit and a snowy white shirt with a striped tie. When his eyes met hers, a warm tingle rushed through her. He took a small box from Chance and started toward her. Dana swallowed back the dryness in her throat as he stopped in front of her.

"You're beautiful," he said.

"Thank you." She took a breath. "You clean up pretty nicely yourself."

He shrugged. "I did some shopping."

She had already known that because he'd taken Evan along with him. Her son had come home the other day, after spending the afternoon in town, acting as if he were hiding a big secret. Then this morning he'd come downstairs dressed in a new suit, white shirt and new shoes. Before she could even comment, he'd scurried to the bunkhouse so Jared could fix his tie. Dana hadn't planned on making such a big deal of the wedding. After all, it was only a business arrangement.

"Thank you again for Evan's suit," she said. "Although, I doubt he'll get much use out of it since he grows so fast."

"It was worth it. He wanted to look good for today. He is my best man." He held the box out to her. "Here, this is for you."

With a puzzled look, she opened it to find a bouquet

of cream- and peach-colored rosebuds. "Oh, my." She reached inside and took hold of the slender stems and raised the bouquet to her nose. "Oh, Jared, they're lovely." Dana started to say more, when the judge and his clerk came in and directed the bride and groom to stand in the middle of the room. Evan took the place on the other side of his mother, Bert next to him.

Jared had Chance as his best man. But this wasn't the small affair they'd planned. Not with the Randell family around. Although quiet, they were all in attendance. Hank and Ella, all three brothers and their wives.

Ten minutes later, the "I do's" had been exchanged and they were pronounced man and wife. Then Jared was instructed to kiss his new bride. That was one thing that they hadn't talked about: "The kiss." And maybe they should have because when Jared's mouth closed over Dana's he didn't hold anything back. He kissed her like he meant it. Full on the lips and with enthusiasm. When he released her and gave her a wink and a grin, she wanted to smash the heel of her shoe into his foot. Instead she smiled as everyone congratulated them. Then Joy and Chance invited everyone back to the Randell home for a reception.

There, Joy had outdone herself. With help from Ella, Hank Barrett's housekeeper, they had set up a banquet on the sideboard in the dining room. A white- and peach-colored, three-tiered wedding cake was center stage on top of a lace-draped table.

Dana was surprised that Joy had gone to so much trouble. Knowing the marriage wasn't real hadn't diminished her friend's enthusiasm. But even surrounded by all the finery, Dana could not let herself believe that she and Jared would live happily ever after.

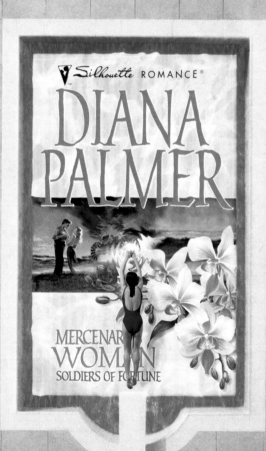

Silhouette authors will refresh you

Silhouette ROMANCE®

DIANA PALMER

MERCENARY'S
WOMAN
SOLDIERS OF FORTUNE

We'd like to send you **2 FREE** books and a surprise gift to introduce you to Silhouette Romance®. Accept our special offer today and

Get Ready for a totally Refreshing Experience!

HOW TO QUALIFY:

1. With a coin, carefully scratch off the silver area on the card at right to see what we have for you—2 FREE BOOKS and a FREE GIFT—ALL YOURS! ALL FREE!

2. Send back the card and you'll receive two brand-new Silhouette Romance® novels. These books have a cover price of $3.99 each in the U.S. and $4.50 each in Canada, but they are yours to keep absolutely free!

3. There's no catch. You're under no obligation to buy anything. We charge nothing—ZERO—for your first shipment and you don't have to make any minimum number of purchases—not even one!

4. The fact is, thousands of readers enjoy receiving books by mail from the Silhouette Reader Service™ Program. They enjoy the convenience of home delivery…they like getting the best new novels at discount prices, BEFORE they're available in stores…and they love their *Heart to Heart* subscriber newsletter featuring author news, horoscopes, recipes, book reviews and much more!

5. We hope that after receiving your free books you'll want to remain a subscriber. But the choice is yours—to continue or cancel, any time at all. So why not take us up on our invitation with no risk of any kind. You'll be glad you did!

SPECIAL FREE GIFT!

We can't tell you what it is…but we're sure you'll like it! A FREE gift just for giving the Silhouette Reader Service™ Program a try!

Visit us online at www.eHarlequin.com

Your FREE Gifts include:
- 2 Silhouette Romance® books!
- An exciting mystery gift!

Scratch off the
silver area to see
what the Silhouette
Reader Service™
Program has
for you.

Silhouette®
Where love comes alive®

YES! I have scratched off the silver area above. Please send me the **2 FREE** books and gift for which I qualify. I understand I am under no obligation to purchase any books, as explained on the back and on the opposite page.

315 SDL DU3Z   215 SDL DU4H

FIRST NAME   LAST NAME

ADDRESS

APT.#   CITY

STATE/PROV.   ZIP/POSTAL CODE

DETACH AND MAIL CARD TODAY!

If offer card is missing write to: Silhouette Reader Service, 3010 Walden Ave., P.O. Box 1867, Buffalo NY 14240-1867

BUSINESS REPLY MAIL
FIRST-CLASS MAIL   PERMIT NO. 717-003   BUFFALO, NY

POSTAGE WILL BE PAID BY ADDRESSEE

SILHOUETTE READER SERVICE
3010 WALDEN AVE
PO BOX 1867
BUFFALO NY 14240-9952

NO POSTAGE
NECESSARY
IF MAILED
IN THE
UNITED STATES

* * *

Jared had been separated from Dana when the ladies commandeered his bride. Something about opening some *personal* gifts. Just as well, he was getting weary of strange women kissing him and giving him those knowing looks.

It was a little late to have doubts about this arrangement. The one thing that bothered him was leaving Dana to face all the probing questions. But they had both known from the beginning that this was the way things would be—strictly business.

Yeah, right. And what was that kiss about? he wondered, recalling Dana's sweet taste. Dear Lord, she looked so beautiful. He'd always thought her pretty, but she had caught him off guard when he'd walked into the judge's chambers. How was he going to keep his hands to himself? Maybe he should stay parked in the bunkhouse. He closed his eyes, remembering how good she felt in his arms. How soft her skin… He took a big swallow of champagne.

"Jared," Evan called as he ran up to him. "Are you my dad now?"

Jared crouched down to the boy's level. "We talked about this before, Evan. I'm your dad's brother, so I'm your uncle." Dana and he had finally told Evan about Marsh just a few days ago.

"But you married my mom," he said.

He knew the boy was too young to understand. "How about for a little while you call me Uncle, but then we'll see what happens."

"'Kay," he said, and ran off to a group of Randell kids.

When Jared stood, Chance came up beside him. "Getting the tough questions already?"

"You can say that," Jared said.

"I had it a little easier," Chance said. "Katie wasn't old enough to ask me questions. But I bet Evan isn't holding back."

"He wants a dad, and I can't blame him. But I don't know how to tell him I might not be around forever."

"None of us can make that kind of promise," Chance countered, then smiled. "You may be surprised how things turn out."

Jared shook his head. "I don't know what I'm doing. I've never had a good relationship with my own father."

Chance's gaze darted away. "There's probably a good reason for that." He looked back at Jared. "The results of the test came back this morning. I don't know if you'll consider it good or bad news, but you're a Randell."

Jared puffed out a breath. How did he feel? At least now he no longer owed any allegiance to Graham Hastings, the man who'd never wanted him in the first place. "I'm almost relieved. It explains so much." He looked at his half brother. "Again, I don't want you to think that I'll expect anything from you or your brothers."

Chance shook his head and grinned. "You sure are one us. You're about as stubborn as a Randell comes. As I said before, we don't give handouts. What my brothers and I would like is to get to know you, Jared. Maybe we can become friends."

Jared had always kept to himself, but found he wanted to get to know the Randells. "I'd like that."

"Just so you know, there are people around here who have a long memory when it comes to Jack Randell. He made some enemies. Some still resent us just because we're his sons. But for the most part, they know that we aren't like our father. We've been lucky. Hank took us in and raised us. He made us walk the straight and narrow before we'd gotten into too much trouble. As far as Cade, Travis and I are concerned, he's our true father."

Just then Cade approached them. "I guess Chance told you the news." He held out his hand. "Welcome to the family. I hope you're not sorry you looked us up."

"Not so far." Jared shook Cade's hand and soon Travis joined them. He, too, offered a welcome. Jared was overwhelmed by how easily the brothers invited him in. If this kept up, he might never want to leave San Angelo.

But of course, he would in the end. He just didn't fit in with family.

Around nine o'clock that night, Jared drove his new bride and son back to the Lazy S. A few days ago he had gotten his truck from the shop. Tonight the cab was quiet, with Evan and Bert both asleep in the back seat, as the soft sound of a country ballad played on the radio.

A single light at the back door greeted them as Jared pulled into the driveway. He got out of the truck, came around and opened the door for Dana.

"I'll carry Evan inside." He helped her out, then reached behind the seat to unfasten the boy from the safety seat. He got a few sleepy groans for his efforts, but Evan didn't wake up. After they said good night to Bert, Dana led the way to the house.

She opened the door and allowed Jared to go first. She followed him upstairs, into Evan's bedroom, and pulled back the covers. Jared lay the child on the cool sheets, and Dana began to strip away Evan's clothing, leaving him in his underwear. She dropped a kiss on his forehead and then she and Jared started out, but Evan called Jared back. When he leaned over the bed, Evan hugged him.

Dana turned away from the touching scene, not want-

ing to think about her quick decision to start a marriage
that was only going to end up hurting her and her son.
She walked out ahead of Jared, then together they continued down the hall past Dana's bedroom. At the end of
the hall, she opened the door to the master bedroom.

"I can't sleep here, Dana. This was your parents'
room."

"There isn't any other room. Besides, this is the only
bed that will be big enough for you."

"Can't you move in here, and I'll sleep in your
room?"

She shook her head. She'd always dreamed of sharing
this room with her husband one day. "No, it's too much
work for a short time. Please, Jared, let's not argue. It's
just a bedroom," she said. When he nodded, she went
on to say, "There are fresh sheets on the bed and towels
in the bath." She pointed to the door across from her
room. "I'm sorry, we'll have to share."

"That's fine." He turned his dark gaze on her, making
her shiver. "I have no problem sharing."

Dana tried to stay indifferent, but that was nearly impossible. The space between them was practically electrified. She could smell the musky scent of his aftershave,
mixed with a little soap. All she had to do was lean a
little closer and she'd be against his hard body. As much
as she tried to deny it, she couldn't stop her own desires.
She had to get away from him.

"Do you need anything else?" she asked, trying to
ease her rapid breathing.

"No, I think I have more than enough."

Dana nodded, afraid to say another word. She then
turned and walked away. Making it safely inside her bedroom, she sank against the raised paneled door and let

the tears fall. She had a right to cry, didn't she? She blamed it on exhaustion of the day. But the big factor was that this was her wedding night and she was spending it alone. When she thought about the beautiful nightgowns she'd gotten at her bridal shower, gowns she'd be the only one to see, more tears fell.

Oh, yeah, she had a right to cry.

The night had been long and sleepless, but in the morning Dana managed to drag herself out of bed. With her head pounding, she pulled on a robe and headed to the bathroom for an aspirin.

She pushed open the door and gasped as she found the room already occupied by none other than her husband.

"Oh, I—I didn't know you were in here," she stuttered, staring at the nearly naked man shaving at the sink. Well, there was a towel covering the vital parts below his waist, but his glorious chest and arms were exposed.

"Don't worry about it. I'm just finishing up." He rinsed off his face and wiped it with another towel. Dana couldn't move if her life depended on it. With his sculptured muscles along his broad chest and long arms, he was absolutely beautiful. A swirl of dark hair covered his chest, barely hiding the flat male nipples beneath.

A warm tingling sensation shot through Dana's body, causing her own nipples to ache and harden into tight buds. She bit back a groan and turned her attention to his face and was met with an intense look.

"I'll come back," she suggested.

"No need, I'm finished now." He walked forward and stopped in front of her. "It's all yours," he said as his gaze swept over her sleepwear.

Embarrassed by Jared's close scrutiny, Dana fought the need to cover herself. She'd been foolish enough to wear one of the new gowns that Joy had given her at the shower. The nearly sheer ivory-colored fabric didn't hide much.

"That's a beautiful gown," he said, desire showing in his eyes. "Did you get that yesterday?"

She pulled the robe together. "Yes, Joy bought it for me." She shrugged. "I thought I might as well wear it."

He edged past her. He was so close, they touched momentarily. "I'd say there isn't much to wear," he said. "But if you want to keep things calm around here, I suggest you not wear this pretty thing again." He tugged on the thin strap on her shoulder. "I'm only human, Dana." He stepped past her and walked down the hall, then disappeared into his bedroom.

Dana wanted to slam the bathroom door. Angry with Jared, and with herself. He was right, she shouldn't have put on the gown last night. Yet she hadn't expected to see Jared this morning. Next time she would cover herself better. Of course, he didn't need to walk around in a towel, either. But she wasn't going to tell him how that affected her.

No, the man didn't need to know how much she was beginning to care about him. Somehow, some way she had to keep her feelings hidden from him.

But how could she fool her own heart?

Chapter Seven

Dana was running late because she'd decided to take a little more care with her appearance on the first full day of her marriage. She applied some makeup, even dressed in a nicer pair of jeans and a bright pink blouse. She hurried downstairs to start breakfast, but came to a halt in the kitchen doorway when she found Jared standing at the stove frying bacon.

Never had she expected to see him cooking in her kitchen. Married! Dana still had trouble believing it. She eyed the man she'd taken as her husband only yesterday. Faded jeans covered his slim waist and long legs. Her gaze traveled upward to the burgundy colored T-shirt that highlighted his perfectly sculptured back and shoulders. Her body temperature suddenly shot up.

"Mom, what are you doing?"

Dana glanced down to see her son beside her. "Oh, nothing, sweetheart. Good morning." She smiled as Jared turned toward them both.

"Morning, sport," Jared said. Then those gorgeous blue eyes settled on her. "Morning, Dana…again."

Another shiver slithered along her spine. "Morning." She walked into the room. "You don't need to cook breakfast. That's my job."

Jared flipped and caught the spatula midair. "Says who? You work as hard as the rest of us, plus cook all the meals. I think the men in the house can manage breakfast. Isn't that right, Evan?"

"Yeah, Mom, I want to help Jared cook." He marched up to the stove. "What do I do?"

Jared took in the boy's wide questioning eyes and realized he was looking to him for guidance. Jared could remember so many times when GH had ignored him. He had no intention of letting Evan down. "How about you set the table while I finish cooking the bacon. Then we'll make some of my special pancakes."

"Oh, boy," Evan said, and hurried to the drawer, pulled out flatware and carried it to the table.

"How can I help?" Dana asked.

When Jared looked at her, hour-old memories flooded his head. A woman with hair wild from sleep, and nearly naked, walking into the bathroom. The nightgown she'd worn was so sheer he could see her rosy nipples trying to poke through the fabric. He had fought the urge to kiss away her shocked expression. He grabbed the towel from the kitchen counter and tucked it in the waistband of his jeans, hoping to hide the effect she had on him.

"Why don't you just sit down and let us men wait on you for a change?"

"Yeah, Mom, let us handle breakfast," Evan repeated as he walked around the table, setting out the utensils at each place. Once finished, he returned to the stove. "Are we ready to make pancakes yet?"

Jared took out the griddle. "We need a few things...."
He went to the refrigerator and opened the door. The cool
air felt wonderful in the warm kitchen. He took out eggs
and milk, then went back to the stove. "Pull up a chair,
son."

Evan did as he was told and together they mixed up
batter. With the boy's help the pancakes took longer and
they weren't anywhere close to perfect. But Evan was so
proud of his accomplishment that it warmed Jared's
heart.

"Look, Mom. Look what I made." Evan climbed
down, took the first stack from Jared, then carefully carried the plate to his mother.

"Oh, they look wonderful. I bet they taste good, too."
Jared watched as Dana poured syrup on the stack, then
took a bite. "Mmm, delicious."

The boy grinned. "She likes them."

"Well, get back over here so we can eat, too."

Evan scurried up on his chair and with Jared's help
they scooped off another four as Bert walked in the door.

"Bert! We're making flapjacks for breakfast."

The foreman hung his hat on the hook by the door.
"Well, *leapin' lizards,* that's my favorite kind of food."

Evan gave him a plate, then with another satisfied cus-
tomer, came back to the stove. Finally they all were sitting around the table eating breakfast.

"Who taught you to cook, Jared?" Evan asked as he
stuffed a forkful of pancakes into his mouth.

"After I left home, I had to learn to feed myself, and
pancakes were cheap and filling."

The boy looked concerned. "Did you ever get lonely?
Bein' by yourself."

Too many times to count, Jared thought. "Yeah, sometimes." He smiled. "But never hungry. Not since I

learned to cook.'' Jared took a big bite of his food. "A man needs to know how to take care of himself.''

"I can make my bed and clean my room. I can feed Sammy and brush him. Oh, and I can hammer a nail real good.'' He smiled with pride. "Now I can make pancakes.''

"I say for a four—almost five-year-old—that's pretty good.''

"I'm going to be five next month. Five more weeks. Bert and me been countin'.'' Evan got up from the table and went to the calendar hanging on the wall. On his tiptoes, he lifted the June sheet and pointed to the twenty-fifth of July. "That's my birthday.''

"I can see that. What is it you want?'' Jared asked.

Evan glanced at his mom, then lowered his head. "I want a horse, but mom says we can't afford one. We need other things.''

Jared didn't know what to say. As much as he wanted to make his nephew's dream come true, he knew enough to stay out of it. "That's true. The Lazy S does need a lot of things.''

"It's okay.'' Evan's head bobbed. "I got what I really wanted already.''

"What's that?''

The child smiled. "For you to be my daddy.''

Her son wanted Jared to be his father. Evan's words played over and over in Dana's head. What a great way to start off a marriage. If it were a real marriage.

Thankfully everyone finished breakfast quickly, and Bert took Evan with him to finish up the morning chores. With the dishes still on the table, Dana waited to clear the table, knowing she and Jared needed to talk.

She took a long breath and released it. "Evan seems

to expect you to be his father. I don't know where he got that idea, Jared. I'll talk with him.''

''Technically I am his stepfather,'' Jared said. ''And at the least his uncle.''

Dana shook her head in disbelief. She had been so careful to explain to her son that Jared would only be staying a little while. That this marriage was only temporary. ''But you're not staying here, nor are we staying married. I don't want Evan to expect you to be around and end up disappointed.''

''I'm not disappearing from Evan's life.''

''It's not the same thing. He's only four years old. He has this notion in his head that he can make you stay.''

''Okay, I'll talk with the boy.''

She nodded, but knew that no matter what, someone was going to get hurt. She could handle rejection, but not Evan.

Jared didn't say anything for a long time, then finally spoke. ''We need to talk about what happened this morning in the bathroom. I know it was a little awkward for you. If my being here makes you uncomfortable, I can move back to the bunkhouse.''

''No,'' Dana said. ''It's fine. I was caught off guard this morning. I haven't had another person around in a long time. If we work up a schedule that won't have us running into each other, we should be okay,'' she offered, feeling a little breathless whenever he looked at her.

''I have no problem with showering in the evenings.''

''I have a bigger concern than our bathroom schedule.''

''What?''

''The Lazy S. I just don't know where to start. I mean I know what I need and what I want to do, but…how much money is available?''

"As much as you're going to need. I contacted the estate lawyer, Russell Janny, this morning. We only need to overnight a copy of our marriage license so the trust money can be transferred into an account in San Angelo. Janny said if there's any problem at the bank to have them call him and he'll guarantee the loan payment. So how would you and Evan like to go into town this morning?"

Dana was happy and nervous at the same time. It wasn't easy for her to trust people. As soon as Jared paid off the loan she'd feel beholden to him. He would be her partner, whether he liked it or not. She bit her lips. "That would make Evan happy."

"What would make you happy, Dana?"

His eyes sparkled mischievously. He'd had that same look when she'd walked into the bathroom. She shook away the picture of the near-naked man, knowing she had to stop thinking this marriage was nothing close to a traditional one. "I'd be happy if I could get rid of the bills and get this place to pay."

"Sounds like a plan. I've been talking with Bert. He tells me that the Western Livestock Auction is in Midland this coming Tuesday. He thinks we should go and look at some stock, especially the bulls." He cocked an eyebrow. "Maybe we could look at some horses, too."

She felt her excitement build, but fought it. "It's a little soon to start thinking about raising horses, or buying Evan a large pet."

"It's your dream, Dana," he said, his voice husky. "And I'm sure Evan wouldn't mind having a mare that you could breed, too. I mean we have six stalls available. So if you find a nice brood mare—I mean…I don't see what it would hurt to look."

She shrugged as if not caring, but her heart pounded

with excitement. "I guess it wouldn't hurt—just to look."

"Good." He stood. "I'm going to talk with Bert. He says he has a lead on a couple of guys looking for work. Might as well hire them and have them finish repairing the fences before we bring in more cattle." He hesitated, then said. "I'll be back around noon, unless you need me for something."

A dozen wild thoughts ran through her head. "No, I'm fine."

He smiled. "Then let's plan on having lunch in town."

She nodded and he walked out the door.

Dana hugged herself as a warm shiver went through her. She hated herself for her weakness…her weakness for her husband. How long could she fight these feelings? More importantly, how long before he walked away? No doubt sooner or later he would, and she'd be alone again.

The following Monday, with Chance and Cade keeping an eye on the Lazy S, Dana, Evan, Bert and Jared all climbed into Jared's truck and headed to Midland for the livestock auction. Over the next two hours, Evan peppered question after question at anyone who might have answers. Jared hadn't minded; in fact he'd enjoyed spending time with the boy.

Every afternoon since he'd started the repairs, Evan had been his shadow. And Jared had put in a lot of hours in the barn. Six stalls had been practically rebuilt, and all had sturdy new gates, ready for the new residents that might take up occupancy real soon. He'd finished the corral as of yesterday so that it could be used for riding lessons.

Jared wouldn't mind if Dana found a couple of mares today. He figured she deserved to have something that she wanted, too. Maybe if she achieved her dream of raising horses, she would begin to smile again. And Dana was so pretty when she smiled.

Jared had talked to Chance about a horse for Evan. His half brother gave him some tips about what to look for in buying a good saddle horse for the boy. Jared just hoped that he could convince Dana that her son was ready.

Arriving in town, Jared stopped at one of the chain motels and got their last two rooms for the night. When they entered one of the connecting rooms, Evan scurried toward the first double bed.

Bert tossed his bag on the other bed. "The boy and I will bunk in here," he said.

Jared glanced into the other room to find a king-size bed. "Sounds good." He set his bag on the floor. He glanced at his wife and said with a quiet voice, "I asked for all doubles, but this was all they had. You want to go somewhere else?"

"No," she said, shaking her head. "It's fine. We should be able to manage for one night."

Jared nodded in agreement, but questioned his sanity. Who was he trying to convince? He watched as Dana moved around the room, putting her things away. He wondered if she'd brought the gown she'd worn the other morning in the bathroom. His body stirred to life. Oh, boy, the problems were starting already. How did he ever think he could stay totally detached from this woman? And how the hell was he supposed to spend the night with her in the same bed and keep his hands to himself?

He needed a miracle.

They ate supper at a steak house next to the motel. Since he wasn't driving, Jared had a few more beers than his usual one glass, hoping that it would help diminish his sexual appetite. But when they returned to the motel, Dana put Evan to bed, then to give Bert some privacy, the door to the connecting room was closed, and Jared knew he was in trouble.

The silence was deafening, and at the same time, it was electrified with awareness between them. All he could think about was stripping out of his clothes and climbing into bed. No, that wasn't exactly true. He wanted her naked and with him in that bed. Damn, he had to stop the direction of his thoughts. Grabbing his bag, he went into the bathroom and took a long cool shower, then dried off and pulled on a pair of sweatpants. When he'd finally come out, he found Dana sitting on the end of the bed, gripping her nightclothes in her fisted hand.

She glanced up at him, but her gaze didn't meet his for long before she looked away. She stood and tried to move around him, but he put a hand on her arm.

"Dana, don't look at me like I'm going to jump you. Give me credit for some self-control."

She pulled out of his grasp. "Excuse me, but this kind of situation is a little strange to me. I'm not used to sharing a room, or a bed with a man. So I'm not exactly sure on how I'm supposed to act." She marched off to the bathroom and shut the door.

Inside, Dana sank against the door and released a long breath. She knew she'd just made a big fool of herself. But how was she going to be able to get into bed with him?

Dana reached inside the shower and turned on the water, hoping the warm water would soothe away her nervousness. It was only one night. She had to keep her mind focused on the auction tomorrow. They were going to find stock for the ranch. She had to be excited about that. Jared even said she could look at horses. Dana stripped out of her jeans and blouse, then her underwear. Pinning her hair up on her head, she caught a glance of herself in the mirror. She'd always been on the thin side. Now her body was more rounded. She had long, firm legs that had a nice shape to them. Her gaze moved to her breasts. They were fuller since she'd had Evan. Her nipples had changed, too. They were darker, a deep rosy color. Her thoughts turned back to Jared again and the tips hardened into tight buds. With a groan, Dana climbed into the shower and cooled the water temperature, hoping to stop her fever.

Twenty minutes later, she came out of the bathroom wearing her usual faded nightshirt and a pair of cotton panties underneath. On the far side of the bed, Jared faced away from her. Dana went to her side, slipped into the bed and turned off the bedside light. The only illumination came through a slight opening in the drapes.

"Glad to see you made it out. I was afraid you'd drowned."

She stiffened, hoping he'd been asleep. "The water felt good."

Jared rolled onto his back. "Dana, I'm sorry about earlier. I had no right to say those things to you. Of course, you should be leery of me. You don't know me that well."

"No, you were right," she admitted, glad that it was dark and he couldn't see her. "I had no reason to act that way toward you. You've been nothing but a gentleman."

There was a long silence, then he spoke again. "Was Marshall... Did he give you cause to be afraid?"

"No. Marshall was always nice to me." She closed her eyes trying to remember the father of her son. "Looking back now, I was the one who'd gone after him. Outside of ranch hands, who came and went, there hadn't been many men in my life. Definitely none as charming as Marshall. I was young and I wasn't exactly experienced. When he gave me a little attention, I practically threw myself at him.''

''I don't think your attention was much of a hardship for my brother.''

Dana didn't know if it was the dark, or Jared's soothing voice that had her admitting things she'd always kept to herself. Even from Joy. ''Thank you. But if Marshall were here, he'd probably say I was a pest.''

Jared rolled over toward her and propped his head in his hand. He was close, so close that Dana could feel his heat. ''Don't sell yourself short, Dana. You're a beautiful woman. Marsh would have never broken his vow to Jocelyn just on a whim. You had to mean something to him.''

He cupped her cheek with his hand, making her turn toward him. Then he lowered his head and touched her mouth with his. The kiss was sweet and tender and over all too quickly. Then he was gone, leaving Dana aching for more.

Dana was dreaming as she turned her face into her lover's shoulder, inhaling his intoxicating scent. Snuggling closer, she brushed her breast against his solid chest and quivered at the contact. Her smooth legs tangled with his rough ones. She stroked her hands up and down his strong arm, then traveled to his broad back.

Dana strained to get nearer and was rewarded when he shifted on top of her. She eagerly opened to him, welcoming his weight. She shivered when he placed open-mouthed kisses along her neck. A gasp escaped her lips when his caressing fingers traced along her thigh, pushing her nightshirt up higher. The sound of his husky voice reverberated against her ear, telling her how much he wanted her.

Dana wanted Jared, too. Jared! Suddenly realization of who she was with and what she was doing hit her. Her eyes shot open. Jared must have sensed her change of mood and raised his head. Neither his blue-eyed gaze nor his body was able to hide his aroused state.

He gave her a crooked smile. "This is a pleasant surprise. Guess the bed wasn't big enough after all."

Dana concentrated on slowing her breathing.

Jared looked down at her. "I guess we need to decide what to do next," he suggested, his voice low, sexy.

How was she supposed to think when his hard body was pressed against hers? She nodded.

His gaze moved to her mouth. "Should I go away, or should I just give in to temptation and kiss that inviting mouth of yours?"

Dana's heart started racing. She wanted his kiss. Oh, how she wanted his kiss. What could one hurt? She closed her eyes just as his lips touched hers.

"Mom! Jared!" Evan called out as the connecting door flew open and they both jerked apart. Jared moved off Dana as she pulled the sheet higher around her.

"Morning, sweetheart," she managed.

"Mom, Uncle Jared, aren't you going to get up?" Her son was already dressed in his new jeans, shirt and boots. The front of his hair had been parted and combed, the back still tangled from sleep. She glanced at the clock. It was six-thirty.

Jared hauled Evan up on the bed. "Hey, sport, give your mom a few minutes. This is kind of a vacation. Not everyone gets up before the sun.'' He tickled the boy, glad that the distraction was cooling him off.

Evan giggled. ''Stop!''

''Only if you go back into your room and give your mom fifteen minutes to get ready. Then we'll go out to breakfast at a restaurant and see if their pancakes are as good as ours.''

'''Kay.'' He climbed off the bed. ''How long is fifteen minutes?''

Jared grabbed the notepad and pencil from the night table. He wrote down a number. ''When this number comes up on the clock, you can come and get us.'' He handed it to Evan and the boy took off. Jared got up and closed the door to give them some privacy.

He turned back to Dana. Big mistake. She looked gorgeous. All mussed up as if she'd been thoroughly loved. But not quite. He released a breath. ''Why don't we just say that what happened here,'' he suggested, motioning to the bed, ''was a slip in judgment.'' When he caught her hurt look, he relented a little. ''I'm sorry, Dana. I didn't mean for this to happen. But a beautiful woman in a man's bed in the morning is a volatile combination.''

Dana turned away. Hell, he couldn't tell her the truth. That he wanted her in his bed. He couldn't give her that kind of power over him.

She got out of bed, her short nightshirt revealing long, shapely legs. He swallowed back a groan as she walked around, gathering the clothes she was going to wear for the day.

Dana stopped and turned to look at him. ''I don't see that there's a problem, since we won't be sharing a bed in the future.'' Her words sounded so final. Then she went into the bathroom and closed the door, leaving Jared aroused and hungry for what he could never have.

Dana Shayne Trager.

Chapter Eight

Evan looked happy as they walked around the stock-yard, and Dana knew the reason. He was with Jared. The man's patience with a four-and-a-half-year-old's unending chatter bordered on sainthood. Of course, earlier in bed, Jared Trager had proven himself far from being a saint.

Dana was still trying to recover from the nearly disastrous mistake. She wanted to blame it on being half-asleep. She'd thought being in Jared's arms had been a dream. But the fiery touch of his hands on her, his hard body against her had been real. A surge of heat and panic rushed through her as she wondered what would have happened if Evan hadn't interrupted them.

"Land sakes, girl, are you hearin' anything I'm sayin'? I've been talkin' to myself for the last ten minutes."

"I'm sorry, Bert." She pulled the program from the back pocket of her jeans. "I guess I didn't get much sleep last night." The minute she said the words she knew what they implied. What could she say? After all, she and Jared were married—newly married.

Bert gave her a grin, then turned toward the large corral to examine the stock. That was what Dana had to do, focus on what she was here for—to stock the ranch with cattle. But one tall good-looking man kept interrupting her concentration.

When Jared and Evan caught up with them, she tried to keep her mind on business. She told Jared about the stock they'd chosen to bid on. He listened intently, then told her that the final decision was hers. It was she who had to make the decision about what was a fair price.

A little nervous, but with Jared by her side during the bidding, she bought two young bulls, along with a dozen heifers and a small herd of yearlings. Although the Lazy S Ranch had always been a mama-and-baby operation, they needed to stimulate some revenue right away.

"Yeah, Mom," Evan cheered, clapping his hands. "We got a whole bunch of calves."

Dana smiled, feeling proud of herself. "Yes, but they aren't pets."

"I know," he said. "Can we go look at the horses now?"

Dana had known this subject would come up sooner or later. She didn't blame her son. She wanted to take a glance to see what was available, too. She glanced at Jared and he winked.

"I think that's a good idea," he said.

With Bert's help earlier, Jared had already looked over the horses. He wasn't an expert, but he knew more about horses than he did cows. Still, as much as he wanted to give Evan a horse, he wasn't going to do anything to upset Dana. It was her decision to make if her son was ready for a horse.

Jared studied the stubborn set of Dana's jaw. So different from this morning when she lay in his arms, so eager for his attention. He could still feel the imprint of her soft body pressed up against him, arching into his touch. His gut tightened when he met her heated gaze. Damn, the woman had him in knots.

He took her by the arm. "Come on," he said, "let's go see some horses."

"I guess it wouldn't hurt to check out the stock," she said.

Once they arrived at the horse corral, they looked around. It was the first time all morning that Evan had been quiet. Jared realized he was very serious about his search. The boy wasn't going to pick a horse out too quickly. Jared admired the almost-five-year-old's maturity. Maybe he was ready to handle the responsibility of ownership after all.

Finally Evan singled one out. "Oh, Mom, look at that horse," he cried.

Dana turned to see her son pointing at a sweet, golden chestnut mare. She eyed the animal closely, admiring her straight back. The mare was well proportioned with no visible abnormalities. She was adorable. Her only drawback seemed to be her small size. But for what Dana wanted, she was perfect.

Then Evan pointed to another horse, a bay filly. She was a beauty with an auburn coat and black mane and tail. This one wouldn't be as easy to take home. Dana had no doubt that this pretty filly would bring a good price.

"She's a beauty, isn't she?" Jared said, coming up to the railing next to her.

"Yeah, she is," Dana agreed, feeling a tingle of heat as his arm brushed hers. "And she'll go for top dollar."

Their eyes held a moment before she looked down at her program, searching over the rest of the horses up for bid. "Too expensive for me."

"You never can tell," he said as he watched Evan go with Bert to look at more horses. "Do you see anything that might work for Evan?"

Dana knew that it was useless to deny the boy. Some way, Jared was going to get her son a horse, so she wasn't going to fight it. "That chestnut mare," she said, pointing at the animal. "She looks like she'd make a good saddle horse. A little small for a full-size man, but perfect for kids."

Jared nodded. "Bert pointed her out earlier. Why don't we circle her in the program and you pick out a few more and see if we can get a good price?"

How many horses was he planning on bidding on? "How many horses do we need?"

"Enough to get you started in your business," he said.

"We can't afford it."

"We can't afford not to," he argued. "It's a business investment, Dana. There's no reason to wait. Besides, Chance mentioned he'd like to offer riding lessons to their guests, but they don't have the room or personnel. This might be your opportunity to work out a deal with the Randells, but you can't if you don't invest in good stock."

Dana knew that was all speculation. And what if she failed? "But the money…"

"I told you the money's not a problem. This is an investment and I know your riding stable is going to take off. With a little more work on the barn, we can take in boarders."

Dana couldn't help but feel excited. "I guess it wouldn't hurt to see what kind of deals we can get."

Jared smiled victoriously. They gathered up Bert and Evan, then they took their seats in the stands. As the time neared, Dana grew more nervous. She didn't want to get her hopes up, because she wasn't going to go crazy with the bidding. She had a limit on what she would spend.

When the little chestnut came up for bid, Evan jumped up. "Look, Mom, there she is. It's Goldie. I want her." He swung around to look at his mother, his expression serious. "And I don't care if other kids ride her. And I promise to feed her, brush her and keep her stall clean."

Goldie. Oh, no, he'd already named the horse. "We'll see, honey." When the auctioneer started the bidding, Dana joined in. As the price began to climb, she hesitated, then she caught the hopeful look in her son's eyes. She lifted her number in the air and held her breath until the auctioneer announced "Sold." Evan cheered and hugged her. She glanced at Jared, and he, too, looked pleased.

A few horses later, the bay filly was led into the corral. She was a beauty tossing her head back and prancing around the ring. With the amount of mumbling going on in the crowd, Dana knew that several people were interested in her. The bidding started a lot higher than Dana had expected and she wasn't going to last long. The big boys were playing, and she wasn't in their league. She tried to hold back her disappointment as she saw the beautiful animal slip from her grasp. Then suddenly Jared took the number from her and raised it when the auctioneer called for more bidding. It went higher still, and he kept up until it began to drop off. Dana remained frozen until the bidding was over and Jared was the new owner of the bay mare.

"Jared! You shouldn't have spent so much money for a saddle horse," she cried.

"I know enough about horseflesh to know an exceptional one when I see it. I have no doubt that she'll produce some great foals. You should talk to Chance about breeding her. Who's to say you can't sell a foal or two?"

"Yeah, Mom," Evan said, his head bobbing up and down. "Jared knows a lot of stuff." The boy grinned. "Now we both have horses. Can we go get Goldie now?"

"Not yet, son," Jared said. "We have more horses to see."

He couldn't be serious. "Jared, no," she said. "You've spent enough."

Jared leaned down and whispered in her ear. "You're cute when you get all bossy. But as long as we're here, we need to concentrate on buying a few good saddle horses. You need at least one more. I've told you to buy what you need."

Dana couldn't believe it. It was like her birthday and Christmas all rolled into one. Was she truly going to be able to open her stable? "Okay," she sighed, "but only one more. If you try to talk me into any more than that, I'm out of here. And remember, you still have to live with me."

Jared tried not to grin. "One more," he agreed, then glanced at Bert. "We better make it a good one."

Dana didn't trust her judgment when it came to men. She just had to put a halt to it before it all got out of control. Ever since Jared appeared in her life, she hadn't been able to control anything, especially her feelings. After this morning, she'd known she'd lost that battle, too.

Jared pulled the truck into the drive around seven that evening. He felt good. He hadn't had this much fun in a long time. He smiled as he looked at Evan in the back seat. He was awake, but barely. The kid had had a busy few days. Jared climbed out, reached into the bed of the truck and took out the bags, then headed to the house.

When Jared came back outside, he saw Chance leaving the barn. He'd stopped by to keep an eye on the place and feed the horses. "How was your trip?" he asked.

"You can tell me tomorrow," Jared said, "when the horses arrive."

Chance frowned. "Horses? You bought Evan more than one?"

"We ended up buying three. One is for Evan, the other two are Dana's. An auburn filly and a dapple gray gelding. I think you'll like the bay. She's a real beauty." He pulled the papers out of his pocket and handed them to Chance.

He looked them over, then released a soft whistle. "She cost you enough, but a classy lady usually does. She came from a good farm and has very impressive bloodlines. It seems a waste to just use her for a riding mount."

"I was thinking the same thing," Jared said. "I suggested to Dana that she might be interested in breeding her with one of your studs."

Chance pursed his lips. "Could be. I'd have to see her first."

"Sounds fair."

"When is she being delivered?"

"Tomorrow afternoon. The livestock is being shipped this weekend. I know I've asked a lot of you already, but do you think you can come by and help unload them?"

A smile tugged at his mouth. "Sure. But don't you worry. I'll get you back. I happen to know you're much better with a hammer and saw than I am."

"No problem," Jared told him. "Say, why don't you bring Joy and Katie with you? We'll barbecue some steaks." Whoa, since when did he do family gatherings?

"Maybe you should check with Dana before you go handing out invitations."

"Ask me what?" The wooden screen door slammed as Dana walked out onto the porch where she found Chance and Jared. They looked so much alike that she wondered why she'd never seen the resemblance before.

"Chance is going to help us unload the livestock on Saturday afternoon. So I invited him and Joy to stay for supper. I thought we'd barbecue."

Dana had never been a couple before. How was she supposed to act? "That sounds…nice."

"Well, you know me," Chance began, "I'll go anywhere for a free meal, but you better call Joy and work out the details."

Chance said goodbye and drove off in his truck. Jared climbed the steps to the porch. "I guess I should have asked you first."

Dana looked up at him. "About what?"

"Inviting people over to the house without talking to you first," he said, tipping his hat back. Funny, lately Dana rarely saw him without her daddy's old worn Stetson. It fit him perfectly. Jared seemed to fit in here perfectly.

He frowned. "If it bothers you we can make it another time."

She shook her head. "No, a barbecue is a good idea. Besides, you know Joy is my friend. I owe her so many meals, I've lost count." Dana smiled. "It should be fun." She turned to go into the house, pushing any foolish thoughts out of her head.

"Dana," Jared called, and she looked back. "I had a great time today. I've never been to a cattle auction."

Why did he have to go and say that? She needed to put space between them. Last night had been dangerous. "And costly," she said.

He laughed. "That, too. But well worth it."

"Yes, I suppose it was."

The deep sound of his laughter sent her pulse racing. If only she could be as playful, but she knew she couldn't without getting hurt when he left.

He sensed her mood change. "What is it, Dana?"

She shook her head.

He came closer. "If it's about what happened in the motel room…"

"No. You're right. This marriage isn't permanent. We can't start something that…"

He moved closer. "I'm only thinking about you, Dana. I don't want you hurt, and I'd hate myself if I caused you any pain. I'm here to help you and Evan, but I can't stay. It's not me. I just don't do family very well."

Dana knew Jared was mistaken. In just a short time he had developed a relationship with his brothers and he'd been a father to her son.

Maybe she should try to convince him that he fit into her family perfectly.… For Evan's sake, of course.

On Saturday, there was all kinds of excitement at the Lazy S Ranch. More than there had been in years, Dana reflected. The cattle trucks pulled in around one o'clock that afternoon and not only was Chance waiting, but his brothers, Cade and Travis, were there to help her and Jared.

It took them just thirty minutes to unload the livestock.

The two bulls were corralled in a temporary pen until the brothers were ready to drive the herd out to pasture.

Dana fed the men lunch, then did up the dishes before she changed to go with them. She walked into the barn wearing jeans, chaps and boots, ready for the ride. Yet she couldn't help but detour down the center aisle to where the three new boarders, particularly the bay filly, took up residence. She opened the gate slowly so as not to spook the young horse, Sweet Brandy. Dana wanted to pinch herself. How did she get lucky enough to own this beauty?

"Easy, girl, I only want to give you some attention." The filly backed away, but stopped as Dana's soft voice began to soothe her. Then Dana took hold of the animal's cloth halter and began to stoke her. "How was your night?" Dana glanced around the stall. It was clean. She smiled, knowing the new ranch hand, Owen, must have been up early. At twenty, he was a hard worker and loved horses. Too bad Dana would lose him when he went back to college in the fall.

The filly nudged against her. "So you like this, huh?" The horse bobbed her head up and down and Dana laughed.

Jared was walking Scout out of the stall when he heard Dana's voice. Her soft, throaty tones sounded like a lover's caress, drawing him to Sweet Brandy's stall. She was stroking the filly and not paying any attention to him. Not since their trip to Midland had he been able to get close to her. Avoidance was the best solution for both of them, but that didn't change the fact that he wanted her. Desire shot though him as his gaze wandered over her shapely bottom and long, slender legs covered in snug jeans. That rich auburn hair was tied back in a braid. His fingers itched to be tangled in the wild strands.

He groaned, causing Dana to turn around. "Jared."

"Hey," he said, and forced a smile. "I see she's won you over, too."

"She did that the second she pranced into the ring." Dana came out of the bay's stall. "Thank you for buying her."

"Like I said, she's a great investment." He shut and locked the gate. "In a few years you'll be able to breed her." He took hold of Scout's reins and started walking.

"Give me a few minutes and I'll be ready to leave." She went into the tack room and came out carrying a saddle and headed toward her mount, a gelding roan named Rex.

She began to saddle her horse. "There's no need for you to come," he said. "We have plenty of help with Owen, Chance, Cade and Travis. And there's Bert, too. What about Evan?"

She paused. "Joy's agreed to watch him. So you're going to have more help with me along. I still run this place. This is my ranch."

Jared tied Scout to the railing and went into the stall. He took the bridle from her and made her look at him. "I'm not trying to take anything away from you, Dana. I only want to make things easier for you. I thought you might want to stay home today."

She folded her arms across her chest. "Well, you thought wrong."

Jared knew he hadn't handled it right. "I know that now. I should have talked it over with you." He watched her blink away tears and before he could talk himself out of it, he placed an arm across her shoulders and drew her to him. "I'm sorry, Dana." The feel of her softness against him caused his body to stir immediately. Damn, she felt good. A flood of memories of their trip to Midland came into his mind, reminding him of how close they'd gotten, how they'd nearly made love. He'd come home vowing to stay away from her. And he'd managed all week. He'd showered at night, stayed out in the barn until as late as possible. The only time they had been together was at mealtime.

"I'll try not to overstep again," he said, and pulled back. Her gaze rose to his as his hand moved down her arm and gripped her hand. "Do you think you can forgive me?"

She blinked, but it didn't erase the passion in the emerald depths. "Just don't let it happen again," she said in a soft throaty tone. And all he could think about was a naked Dana against crumpled sheets.

His grip tightened. "I'll try."

"See that you do," she said weakly.

His resistance was faltering. Leaning down, his lips touched hers, then he chanced another nibble and another. With each one of Dana's breathy gasps, his reserve faltered, then disappeared altogether and he covered her mouth completely. He pulled her against him, tilting her back and deepened the kiss. Coaxing her lips apart, he tasted her again and again.

Her arms went around his neck, fingers combed through his nape, causing his hat to fall to the ground, forgotten.

It wasn't until he heard the sound of the men's laughter that he pulled back, but didn't release her.

"Hey, you'll have to save that for later," Chance called out. "We need to ride out before the sun roasts us."

Feeling the heat rise in her face, Dana buried her head into Jared's chest. How could she let this happen? Still trembling from the kiss, she couldn't look at Jared.

He had other ideas. "Dana," he said, cupping her chin and raising her head. "We better go. I'll saddle your horse."

She stopped him. "I don't really need to go. I could use the time to bake a few pies for the barbecue."

He grinned. "Now, I'm not going to argue with you on that one. I just want you to know that I'm not trying to exclude you. I just want to make things easier."

Little by little he was stealing her heart. "Thank you."

"You're welcome." He picked up his hat and started to leave, then stopped. "I'm sorry that Chance caught us, but I'm not sorry that I kissed you." He tugged on his hat, then led Scout out to the corral.

Dana somehow made her way back to the house and found Joy at the kitchen table, drinking her tea. "I thought you were going with the guys to move the new herd."

"I changed my mind."

Joy raised an eyebrow. "By the looks of you, I'd say one carpenter-cowboy may be changing it for you."

Dana's hand went to her hair and realized half her braid was pulled out. She could still taste him on her lips, too. She had no willpower when it came to the man. With a groan, she sank into a chair. "I'm in big trouble."

Joy smiled. "Why is that?"

"Because I'm starting to care about Jared."

"And why is this bad?"

"Because he doesn't feel the same about me, and besides, he'll be leaving soon." *And I'll be alone again,* she cried silently.

"Maybe he doesn't want to leave. He does have family here. Not just Evan, but Chance, Cade and Travis."

Dana shook her head. "He tells me all the time that

he has a life in Las Vegas. That's where he's buying a company."

Joy reached across the table and patted Dana's hand. "I think Jared is fighting the feelings he has for you. He could change his mind about leaving. I remember Chance after we first were married. Oh, how he fought to stay away from me. I knew he only married me to get my land, and I needed his protection so I wouldn't lose Katie to my in-laws. But when I realized that I didn't want our marriage to be in name only, I decided I had to take matters into my own hands and let him know how I felt."

Dana was definitely interested. "How did you do that?"

"I seduced him," Joy said proudly. "A bad storm helped out. A tree branch broke the window in my bedroom, and I saw my opportunity and went for it. I went to his bed and persuaded him to share it with me." Her friend looked at Dana. "First, you have to admit that you love Jared. Do you?"

Dana didn't want to say the words out loud, but staying silent didn't change the fact. "Yes, I do," she sighed.

"Then it's simple. Let Jared know how you feel. Show him no mercy and go after him."

Chapter Nine

Go after him.

Dana spent the morning preparing food for the barbecue, but her thoughts kept wandering back to her
friend's words. This was crazy. She'd tried going after a
man once, and look what had happened. She was left
alone with a broken heart. A slow smile spread across
her face. Not completely alone. She couldn't imagine her
life without Evan. He was the joy of her life.

She sobered. Gone was that young, foolish girl. A
mother now, she also had the responsibility of running
the ranch. She couldn't take that kind of risk again. It
was best to leave things as they were—to stick to their
agreement—marriage in name only. She'd rather have
Jared as Evan's uncle and her friend, than to drive him
off completely by trying to hold him here. And besides,
who said Jared was even interested in her? They'd only
shared a few kisses. Surely a man like Jared would prefer
a more sophisticated woman.

"Dana, the oven timer went off," Joy said.

The buzzing sound grew louder. "Oh, what?" Dana finally looked up.

"Your pies are ready."

Dana flushed as she went to the oven and opened the door to find two apple pies, the fillings bubbling through the slits in the golden brown crusts. With oven mitts, she lifted them out, placing them onto the cooling rack as a spicy cinnamon fragrance filled the room.

Just then the back door opened and Chance and Jared walked in. Dusty and dirty from the trail ride, they hung their hats on the hook and went to the sink. Jared pulled two glasses from the cupboard and handed one to Chance to fill. They drank thirstily, leaning against the counter. Both men were broad-shouldered and muscular, but slim-waisted and long-legged. And both Randells were wickedly handsome. In just the short weeks that Jared had been at the ranch, he'd come to look as much like a rancher as Chance did, who'd been born to it.

"You two look beat," Joy said.

"It's hot as blazes out there," Chance said as his wife came up to him. Ignoring the dirt, she kissed her husband as Chance placed his hand on her slightly rounded stomach. "But it was a great workout for my cutters. Dang, you should have seen Owen handle Roughneck. That kid is a natural on a horse."

"Good, but he's only here for the summer." Dana looked at Jared to find that his gaze was on her. She felt her skin warm and wished he'd greet her a little more affectionately. Of course, they didn't need to put on a show for the other couple, even if Chance had caught them kissing in the barn.

"Did things go okay?" Dana asked him.

Jared nodded. "The herd is happily grazing in the north section."

"Good." She turned to Chance. "Where are Travis and Cade?"

"They've already headed home," Chance said, then looked back at Jared. "Hey, you'd be wise to give your wife another big kiss. Take a look at the counter and see what's coolin'."

Jared glanced in the direction Chance pointed at, then at Dana and smiled. "I knew I had a good reason for you to stay here." He came toward her and Dana stiffened as he leaned down and brushed his mouth against hers. She was quite disappointed when he pulled away.

"Thanks for the pies," Jared whispered as their eyes met.

His pulse raced as it had most of the morning. Funny, he'd been the one to convince her to stay home, and then wished she'd been with them. He couldn't resist her any longer and drew her close, even happier when she didn't pull away.

"Dana, you'd be proud of Jared today," Chance announced. "He did good for a *city* boy."

"Thanks." Jared accepted the good-natured ribbing. "But I've spent time on a ranch."

Chance barked with laughter. "A fancy dude ranch isn't my idea of hard work."

He frowned. "A few years back I worked for a large operation outside of Denver. So I've spent my time in a saddle."

"But you'll probably have a few sore places tonight. Just have Dana rub on a little ointment."

Jared tried to keep it light, but the thought of Dana's hands on him had his body reacting. "Not a bad idea."

"Okay, guys," Joy broke in. "I think you both need to clean up and start the grill for some of that good Texas beef."

The sound of footsteps on the stairs told them the kids were close. Evan ran into the room, Katie close on his heels. The little girl ran to her daddy.

"Uncle Jared, you're back." Evan's eyes lit up as he ran to him. "Can you take me riding on Goldie?"

Jared crouched down. "Evan, we've talked about this. Your mother has to check out your new horse first."

The boy lowered his eyes. "Oh, I forgot." He looked up at his mother. "Mom, is it time to eat yet? I'm hungry."

The room broke into laughter. "I guess it's unanimous," Jared said. "Give me ten minutes to shower and we'll get this party started. Chance, you're welcome to use the bathroom downstairs."

His half brother shook his head. "My things are in the bunkhouse, I'll just use the shower there."

Jared nodded. They'd been strangers a month ago. Now they were becoming friends. "Thanks for today, Chance. I really appreciate it."

"That's what family is for."

It was funny, the steaks were the easy part of the meal. Dana watched through the kitchen window as Jared and Chance stood by the grill, long-neck bottles of beer in their hands, talking about the exploits of the morning's cattle drive.

But the kids playing in the yard weren't to be ignored. Before long, Jared and Chance put down their drinks and took turns tossing the children the ball, praising every time one of them made a catch, encouraging them when they didn't. The laughter was contagious.

"That's the sweetest sound," Joy said.

"What?"

"A child's laughter," her friend said. "It's so innocent, so carefree. There's nothing like it in the world. That's one of the reasons I fell in love with Chance. The way he was with Katie. They say that kids and animals are great judges of character.'' She nodded to Jared as he bent down, showing Evan how to grip a plastic baseball.

Something tightened around Dana's heart. What's not to love? The man gave her son so much attention and affection.

"They're crazy about each other," Joy added.

Dana looked away. "Jared *is* Evan's uncle."

"It's possible that the man wants to be more."

Dana shut her eyes a moment. She couldn't let herself dream that dream. "I just have to take it day by day."

The men finally got the steaks and the kids' hot dogs grilled. Bert and Owen begged off and took their food back to the bunkhouse to kick back and watch television. So it was the two couples sitting at the table, with the two kids happily at a little table of their own. Jared had worked most of the week finishing a small patio area next to the house. He hadn't had time to make the cover, but an oversize umbrella shaded everyone from the late-afternoon sun.

Jared sat back, enjoying the company of the people around him. He couldn't remember ever having a Hastings family barbecue. Funny, he'd only known Chance, Joy, Dana and Evan for such a short but they were more family than he'd ever known. There were times, like today, when he wanted to fit in. And he would miss this when he left.

He stole a glance at Dana and recalled the kiss they'd shared in the barn. There were a lot of other things he would miss. Like seeing Dana the first thing in the morning with her eyes still hooded from sleep, and her hair hanging loose....

Dana got up to tend to the children. His attention went to the white shorts she had on. The day was a hot one and it was getting hotter by the minute. He shifted in his seat as his gaze examined her rounded bottom and long legs. Her sandals exposed small narrow feet, with dots of pink polish on each toe. She wore a tank top that high-lighted her trim arms with enough muscle to show she was in shape. Ranching was hard work, and Dana didn't slack on her duties. She worked just as hard as the rest. He wished she didn't have to. The consolation was that she loved the ranch. He had to admit that he, too, was enjoying the time he spent on the Lazy S. And the time he had with Evan and Dana.

Chance patted his flat stomach. "That apple pie was top-grade choice." He winked. "Dana, as long as you have pie, you can ask me for help anytime."

Dana smiled. "So that's Joy's secret way to get you to do things."

Chance grinned at his wife. "Let's just say it's one of the ways."

Jared watched the couple exchange an intimate look. It was almost if everybody else around had disappeared. They were so unaware of anyone but each other. Damn, he envied that.

Dana's eyes locked with his and heat surged through him. He thought about how much he wanted to kiss her again. Right now, right here. He knew it was more than he had a right to, but he couldn't help it.

Dana was taking longer than usual putting Evan down for the night. And of course the child wasn't cooperating.

"But I'm not tired," he argued. "I want to stay up. Please…" He stopped and yawned.

"How about a story?" she asked.

"I want Uncle Jared to read to me," he demanded.

"I'm sorry, but he's busy. I can read to you." She started to pull out his favorite book, *Mike Mulligan and His Steam Shovel*.

"That's a baby book." Evan pouted.

"Hey, partner, you giving your mother a bad time?"

They both looked to the doorway where Jared stood. "Uncle Jared, Mom says you're too busy to read to me."

"Well, I did have some chores to take care of, but I'm finished now." He pushed away from the doorway and walked into the room. "Maybe I can take over for your mom."

"Yeah, you can read me a story."

Dana gladly gave him the book. Their hands touched, sending electrical shock waves through her. Dana turned and kissed Evan good-night, then went downstairs and outside. The mess from the barbecue had been cleaned up and the chairs put away. Jared had been busy.

A cool breeze caught Dana's hair and brushed strands against her face. She pushed them back and released a long breath, trying to banish Joy's words from her head.

Let Jared know how you feel.

She thought about Jared's touch…how his kiss made her skin tingle. Her body was wound tight, and aching for something she knew could hurt her. It had been so long since a man had wanted her. Having Jared around just made her more aware of that fact. She knew that he wasn't going to be here for much longer, so why was she wasting precious time?

"Dana…"

Dana turned around when she heard Jared's voice. He

didn't say any more as he moved across the deck and stopped in front of her. Silently he cupped her jaw, leaned down and pressed his mouth against hers. The kiss was soft and achingly tender, and she wanted it to go on and on.

"Jared..." She didn't realize she'd spoken his name until he broke the kiss.

"What is it, darlin'?" He smiled. "Tell me what you want."

Her heart raced so fast she didn't think she had the breath to speak. "You..."

She barely got the words out before his mouth was back on hers in a searing kiss. His tongue moved into her mouth, dueling with hers, asking for more. His hands caressed her back, then moved to her breasts. She gasped when his fingers teased her nipple through her T-shirt.

"You want me to stop?"

"No, oh no," she whispered.

Jared had reached his limit. He wasn't going to walk away this time; he couldn't. He started to take Dana into the house when he heard his name again. This time it was a male voice.

He broke off the kiss, but cradled Dana against him. He turned to see an embarrassed Owen at the edge of the yard. "I'm sorry to disturb you, Jared, but I need to talk with you."

Jared looked at Dana. "Why don't you go inside and I'll see what Owen wants?"

Dana nodded and left as Jared walked toward the ranch hand. "What is it?"

"Bert would be angry if he knew I'd come to get you...."

"Come and get me? Why? What's wrong with Bert?"

"I think he's hurt. He slipped and fell."

Jared took off toward the bunkhouse. He kept his gait at a quick efficient walk, trying not to worry Owen. What had the old man tried to do? Too much probably.

Inside the long room, he found Bert sitting at the table. "Hey, Bert. I hear you took a fall."

The older man glared at young Owen standing in the doorway. "Looks like someone has a big mouth. I told the boy not to disturb you and Dana." Bert absently rubbed his arthritic knee.

"Owen was just worried."

"No need. I've fallen before."

Jared didn't want to overstep his boundaries. "You want me to call your doctor?"

The foreman gave him an incredulous look. "And he's just gonna tell me what I already know, that my knee isn't worth the powder to blow it up." He turned away. "Said I need to have one of those fancy surgeries."

Jared wondered if Dana knew about this. "Maybe he can give you something for the pain."

"I have a box full of painkillers. Makes my head fuzzy. I can't work like that."

"Why don't you take one to help you sleep tonight? The effects should be worn off by morning."

They finally got Bert to agree, and after one pill, Jared helped him into bed, promising himself that he'd talk with the doctor in the morning.

On the way back to the house, Jared's thoughts returned to Dana. Damn, it had been nearly an hour since he'd told her that he would be right back. He closed his eyes momentarily, recalling how close they'd come... Maybe it was better this way. He would only hurt Dana in the end.

He went into the house, shut off all the lights and went upstairs. Dana's bedroom door was closed and no light shone under the door. Pulling his shirt from the waistband of his jeans, he walked to his room and went inside. There was a soft glow from the lamp beside the bed and he froze when he discovered Dana sitting on top of the blanket. She was wearing a sheer gown and her hair was lying wild against her shoulders.

He began to tremble. "Dana…"

She smiled. "Hi." Her greeting was breathy.

"What are you doing here?"

She rose and walked toward him. "I'm waiting for you," she whispered. "What took you so long?"

"Just a little problem Bert needed help with."

"Is everything okay?"

"It is now."

She raised her arms and placed them around his neck. "Good. Then you don't have to leave again."

Her breath whispered against his mouth and she kissed him. He remained motionless, trying to hide his torment. She pulled back to look up at him.

"And Evan's asleep so I don't have to leave, either. Unless you don't want me here," she said.

Jared closed his eyes as desire ripped through him. Of course he wanted her here. He wanted her so badly, he hurt. But he said, "Maybe this isn't such a good idea. I mean now that…we've had a chance to think about…" She raised up and pressed her body into his, then her hands moved over his chest. He couldn't take any more. "Dana…"

She stopped and looked up at him, her green eyes dilated, her face flushed, her mouth so tempting. His body instantly grew hard.

"Are you saying you don't want me?" she asked.

"No," he breathed. "But I don't want you to have any regrets later."

Her finger touched his mouth to stop his words. "I don't want to think about anything but you right now." She drew a ragged breath. "Jared, I want to be your wife...for as long as we have together."

She took hold of his hand and led him toward the bed. In the dim light, Dana stood before him. Her fingers were shaking as she slowly reached for the gown straps and slid them off her shoulders. Jared's breathing stopped as he watched the feathery fabric leisurely float to the floor.

"I want you to make love to me."

Dana's heart drummed in her ears as the seconds passed. She found herself wanting to cover herself as Jared just stared at her. She knew she wasn't a raving beauty. She was more muscular than the average woman. Maybe her body wasn't as perfect as those he'd been used to.

Unable to stand Jared's apparent lack of interest any longer, she grabbed for her gown. "Sorry, I won't bother you again."

"No, Dana, wait." He reached for her. "Don't ever doubt that I want you. But I'm trying to be noble here and you're making it damn difficult."

"You want me?"

"More than my next breath," he admitted and swept her into his arms.

In a single motion he claimed her lips; his tongue plunged inside. She eagerly accepted the invitation and tasted him, too. Skimming his hands over her shoulders, then down her back, he cupped her bottom as he drew her closer. She moaned softly as so many feelings rushed through her, thrilling and frightening her at the same time.

Jared's chest heaved. "Dana, this is your last chance to change your mind."

Her only comment was her hands going to his shirt and stripping it off his shoulders. "I think you have too many clothes on." Once the shirt was disposed of, she went to his belt and removed it. Then she paused and placed a few kisses against his chest.

Seconds later, his boots and jeans joined his shirt on the floor. He jerked back the blanket and laid Dana down on the cool sheets, then stretched out beside her. She'd never been like this with a man before. They were both exposed, but she realized she trusted Jared and felt safe with him.

With one long finger, he traced the curve of her breasts. "Perfect."

She returned the favor and trailed her finger over his chest, toying with his hard nipple. She was delighted when he made a low guttural sound of pleasure.

Jared was losing control fast as he closed his eyes under the assault of Dana's hands and mouth.

He pushed her on her back and rose over her. "It's my turn," he said as he let his fingertips whisper over her breasts, causing her to moan. Her nipples hardened instantly. "You like that?" He leaned down and circled one tight bud with his tongue, then teased it with his finger.

"Yes…" she breathed, arching her back, so he would repeat the pleasure.

Jared smiled. Dana might have been the one to entice him into bed, but he doubted there had been a man in her life since Marsh. It took everything he had in him, but he needed to go slow with her. Protect her.

Protection.

He grabbed his jeans off the floor and pulled a condom out of his wallet. Once he prepared himself, he came back to her.

"Look at me, Dana." She did. "What we're doing is crazy, but I want you too much to stop." Brushing her legs apart, he moved over her. He grasped her hands and laced his fingers with hers.

"I've wanted you from the first moment I saw you." He stared into her green eyes, knowing she was the most dangerous kind of woman. She was sexy as hell, but wanted more from a man than just a brief mating.

Jared's breathing grew ragged as he leaned down and nipped at her mouth, then down her neck to her breasts again. She whimpered and rotated her body against his, causing him to lose control. His hand moved down between her legs. Feeling her wetness, he slowly pressed into her sweet body.

Dana wanted Jared so badly she couldn't think straight and didn't bother to try. He filled her so completely, nothing had ever felt so wonderful.

He moved agonizingly slow. "Please," Dana cried, knowing she could never get enough of him.

"You want more?" he whispered against her lips.

"Oh, yes." Dana writhed beneath him, then locked her legs around his hips to let him know that she wanted all he had to give. Jared didn't disappoint her. With each stroke, he coaxed her until her body tightened in pleasure and finally her shuddering release tossed them both over the edge. With one last groan, Jared collapsed on top of her, then rolled away, pulling her to his side.

Only their rapid breathing interrupted the silence as Jared felt the damp weight of Dana against him. He was still trying to recover from their lovemaking, but doubted he ever would.

Damn, he had to have been crazy to let this happen. It was going to be hard enough to walk away as it was, now it was nearly impossible. She made him dream of things he couldn't have.

Jared got out of bed and grabbed his clothes. "I'll be right back." He took a trip to the bathroom, then returned dressed in jeans. He stood just inside the door, afraid that he wouldn't be able to leave if he got too close.

"Dana, maybe we acted a little rash here. I should spend the night in the bunkhouse."

Dana sat up, exposing her naked body to him. "Why?"

He sucked in a long breath. How could he want her again so soon?

She leaned against the pillow, but refused to cover her sweet little body. "Are you saying that you don't want to come back into bed…with me?"

He raked his fingers through his hair. "You know that's not true, Dana."

"Prove it."

Dana didn't live in the real world. "You know I'm going to be leaving soon."

Wrapped in a sheet, she climbed out of bed and crossed the room. "You're not leaving tonight, are you?"

He fought to keep from backing away. "No, not tonight."

Dana gave him a slow, sexy smile. "Then come back to bed." She reached for his hand. "I don't want to sleep alone."

Jared resisted with his last ounce of strength. "If I do, I'll make love to you again."

"That's perfect, because I want you to. Unless you're not in the mood."

He didn't answer her question, just swung her up in his arms and carried her back to bed.

Damn, he was going to be tired in the morning, but he was looking forward to it.

Chapter Ten

The bright sunlight streamed through the window, across the bed and right into Dana's eyes. She rolled away, wanting to go back to sleep, but there was no escaping the sun's glare. Which was strange since her room faced the west. Suddenly, memories of last night flooded her head. She gasped and sat up, grabbing the sheet to cover her nakedness.

Naked!

Dana glanced around and realized she was in her parents' bed—no, Jared's bed. Alone. The clock read eight twenty-five. Oh, no, she'd slept through breakfast. Wrapping the sheet around her, she ran to her bedroom. After grabbing some clean clothes, she went to shower.

Why hadn't Jared wakened her this morning? Her thoughts turned to last night and her body warmed in remembrance. Jared had made love to her two more times. Neither one of them had thought much about sleep until he curled up behind her somewhere around 2:00 am.

Now, it was almost nine. Dana, dressed in jeans and a

red blouse, headed downstairs. A little nervous, she realized she didn't know exactly how to behave. How would Jared act toward her? Suddenly she didn't feel as brave as she had just twelve hours ago when she'd lured him to bed. Seeing the empty kitchen, she was happy for the temporary reprieve, but finding the stack of dirty dishes in the sink didn't feel that great.

Deciding she couldn't hide out all day, Dana walked out the back door and headed to the barn. Once inside the cool interior, she started down the center aisle, passing the newly built stalls. That was when she heard Jared's voice. Her breath quickened at the memory of his lovemaking and the familiar, deep-throated tone with which he relayed his need and encouragement to her. The man not only had bedroom eyes, but a voice to match. She hung back until he finished his instructions to Owen, taking the opportunity to check on Sweet Brandy.

Dana went inside the stall. "Well, how are you this morning, Miss Brandy?" she crooned as she stroked the horse's face. Brandy shifted closer. "You want some attention, don't you?"

"Don't we all?"

Dana turned to find Jared at the gate. "Hi," she said. He looked wonderful, wearing faded jeans, a chambray shirt and an old Stetson. Heat rushed to her face as she thought about how he looked without those clothes. She glanced away.

"Good morning," he greeted her.

She forced a smile to cover her nervousness. "I almost missed the morning part. Why didn't you wake me?"

"I did," he said, his smile spreading. "You told me to go away."

Dana couldn't imagine ever telling him to go away. Her body tingled, making her aware that she still wanted him. "I shouldn't have slept so late," she said. "There's work to be done."

Jared shrugged. "Isn't that the reason we hired Owen? So you didn't have so much to do."

"Still, the day starts at sun up."

"I think after last night you need some rest."

Jared watched a blush spread over her face as she avoided his gaze. Did she regret last night? He cursed himself. No matter how much he'd wanted her—still wanted her—he should have been the one to walk away from the temptation.

"Look, Dana. About last night…I don't want you to think that I expect…or take for granted that…"

Suddenly Dana's back straightened as anger flashed in her emerald eyes. "I told you before, Jared. The last thing a woman wants is to hear a man apologize, especially after they made love. And I sure as hell don't need your pity." She tried to push past him, when he stopped her.

"You think that's what I'm doing?" he asked. "You think I made love to you *three* times last night because I felt sorry for you?" He bit back a curse. "I'm fighting everything in me not to pick you up and carry you back to that bed right now."

With a gasp, her eyes rounded.

"Yeah, I want you, all right," he said. "Just like I wanted you this morning. It was hell leaving that warm bed, leaving your sexy, naked body." His voice lowered. "When all I wanted to do was to make love to you again."

"But I thought… I didn't want you to think that you had to—"

Jared pulled her against him, his hands cupping her face. "I think it's time I shut you up before you get yourself into any more trouble." His mouth captured hers in a hungry kiss. He parted her lips and drove his tongue inside to taste her intoxicating sweetness. She whimpered as her body sank against him.

He broke off the kiss, knowing he had to keep his head. "Woman, you're going to get us into trouble."

She smiled. "I've been told that before." She wrapped her arms around his waist. "So what are you going to do with me?"

He groaned, then moved her back. "I think the only safe thing is to keep you at a safe distance."

She pouted. "That's no fun." She started to go to him again when Evan came racing down the aisle.

"Mom, you woke up."

"Yes, I did." Dana bent down and hugged her son. Her fingers combed Evan's unruly hair. It had a crooked part in the front and his curls were slicked down with hair gel. No doubt Evan's handiwork.

"Uncle Jared said you were tired from cooking yesterday."

She glanced at the man who had caused her fatigue. He gave her a wicked grin, stealing her heart all over again. "I guess I was. What have you been doing all morning?"

"I've been taking care of Bert. His knee hurts. So I've been reading him my books."

Dana knew that Evan had memorized his favorite stories. "That's nice of you." Dana shot a look at Jared. "What's wrong with Bert?"

"He fell last night. I guess his knee has been giving him trouble for a while now. I told him to stay off it until I get him to the doctor."

"Why didn't you tell me last night?"

Jared looked down at the boy. "Evan, why don't you

go get Goldie's halter from the tack room? Then we'll see if Owen can exercise her.''

''Oh, boy.'' Evan cheered and scurried off.

Jared's attention turned back to Dana. ''I didn't tell you because Bert asked me not to. He knew you would worry.''

''Of course I'd worry. He's family.''

''I was going to tell you this morning, but I had enough to deal with trying to get Bert to agree to go to the doctor. I'm taking him in to see an orthopedic specialist tomorrow.''

Dana couldn't believe that Bert had agreed to this. She had been trying for months. ''He's letting you take him in,'' she said. She started off toward the bunkhouse, but Jared caught up with her.

''Let him be, Dana. Bert doesn't want a woman feeling sorry for him.''

''But it's my job....''

''And I'm your husband,'' he said, then stepped closer. ''Unless you don't want my help.''

Dana felt the familiar heat of his body and she wanted to melt into him. She'd had to handle things for so long on her own. It would be so easy to give in, but how long would he be around for her? ''I guess I don't have a problem with you helping out.''

Jared smiled. ''Now, did that hurt so much?'' His mouth brushed over hers and she moaned, rising up on her toes for more. He pulled back, his gaze never leaving her. ''You want more?''

''Yes...''

''You're a greedy woman.'' He leaned down and took another nibble, causing more incredible sensations. ''I guess I'll just have to work harder tonight at satisfying you.''

She blinked, unable to hide her reaction.

He stared at her. "Will you have a problem with sharing my bed?"

A shiver went through her. "No," she breathed.

"Good," he said, then lowered his head again and captured her mouth in a bone-melting kiss.

The next day, Dana went outside to greet Jared and Bert as they returned from the doctor. The older man didn't look happy.

"Well, isn't anyone going to tell me what happened?" she asked, staring at the two sullen men.

Jared let Bert talk. "They want to do surgery and replace my knee with a plastic one." He looked at Jared. "I told you before we went that's what they wanted to do. Do you know how much that costs? Too much." He turned around and limped off.

Dana couldn't hide her concern. "There's nothing else they can do?"

"It's the best option. There's medication, but Bert says it makes him drowsy. Says he'll handle the pain."

"How much is the operation?"

"Medicare will take care of most of it, but you know there are always costs." He paced. "I have money for the surgery. All I need to do is figure a way to get him to take it."

Her love for Jared was growing in leaps and bounds. "Bert's a proud man and I love him like a father. He was the only one who helped me after my own father died. Oh, Jared, we've got to help him."

He drew her into his arms. "Somehow I'll convince him to have the surgery."

"Thank you," she whispered. "I don't know how I can ever repay you."

"There's no need. Like you said, Bert is family."

Just then Dana saw a familiar truck pull into the drive. Chance Randell. "I didn't know Chance was coming by today."

"I called him. He's going to help me with some ideas on designing the new horse corral. If you're going to teach riding I thought you might like some special features."

When did these plans come about? she wondered. "And where is this corral going to be?"

"Just on the other side of the barn. It'll be out of the way, but close enough to where the horses are stabled. If you want, you can talk with Chance."

Dana watched as Jared's half brother got out of the truck. She was glad that the two were getting along so well. Deep down she'd hoped that their growing relationship would be another tie to keep Jared in Texas. Secretly she wished she could be enough to make him stay.

"You two can talk now," Dana said, "but invite Chance for lunch and we'll discuss things in detail then."

Jared leaned down and placed a quick kiss on her mouth. "See you later." With a sexy wink, he walked off.

Feeling giddy, Dana went back into the house and busied herself preparing lunch. Since she had the time, she put together a green salad and made egg salad for sandwiches. For an extra treat, she put a peach cobbler into the oven. After setting the table, she started to go get the men when the phone rang.

"Lazy S Ranch," she said into the receiver.

"Hello. I'm looking for Jared Trager," an unfamiliar voice said.

"He's here, but outside," Dana said. "May I take a message or have him call you back?"

"Yes, please. I'm Nate Peterson from Burke Construction. It's urgent that I speak to him."

Dana copied down the phone number Mr. Peterson gave her, then headed out to the corral. She walked through the barn, worried that the "urgent" message would take Jared away from her and Evan. But she had to give it to him. If he was going to stay, he had to make that decision on his own.

She found Jared and Chance standing in the newly mowed area that Jared had cleared just days ago. Coming up behind them, she was about to speak when something Chance was saying stopped her.

"Dana owns a real sweet section in Mustang Valley. You could add some cabins and Dana could move her stable of riding horses over, too. It would make money for all of us."

Jared was surprised at Chance's offer. So, Chance wanted to include him in the Randell business, the Mustang Valley Guest Ranch. Jared knew that it could possibly be the best investment to help supplement the Lazy S. Before he could respond, he caught movement out of the corner of his eyes. He turned to find Dana standing behind him. By the look on her face, she had already heard Chance's ideas.

"Dana, I didn't think you were going to come out."

"It's a good thing I did, or you might have decided to give away all the Shayne land." She shoved a piece of paper at him. "There's an urgent call from Las Vegas, a Nate Peterson." She turned and marched off.

Jared glanced at Chance. "I think you need to explain things to her."

Chance raised his hands in surrender. "I doubt she's ready to listen. She still thinks I want her land."

"Then you're going to have to convince her otherwise."

"You deal with Dana," Chance said. "I've been around long enough to know that whatever I say to her now isn't going to matter." He strolled off toward his truck.

Jared didn't want to argue with Dana, but he had to confront her and he had a feeling she wouldn't make it easy for him. He hurried inside to find her in the kitchen. "Whatever you're thinking, stop. I'm not hooked up with the Randells to get you to sell."

"You couldn't anyway. I own the Lazy S."

"I know that," he said, trying to control his anger. "Believe me, I was as surprised as you were when Chance offered me—offered us—the opportunity to be a part of the Randell corporation. He said his brothers only asked us to come in because I'm family. And there is no selling of any land. Just a chance to be a part of the Mustang Valley Guest Ranch. And since everyone contributes with their own unique skills, Chance was hoping you would want to bring in the riding stables."

Jared watched a speechless Dana mull over the idea. "Don't let your stubbornness stop you from making a good investment." He walked out of the room and into the study, still stinging that Dana didn't believe him. The past weeks together, they'd shared the work, the meals…and a bed. Everything but the most important: trust.

He picked up the phone and dialed Burke Construction. He'd been checking in twice a week, Mondays and Fridays. Thanks to his sexy wife it was Tuesday and he hadn't thought a thing about the construction company.

The phone rang twice before it was answered. "Burke Construction," Nate said.

"Nate. It's Jared."

"Hey, man, sorry to have to do this, but I got some bad news. Stan had a heart attack last night."

Jared closed his eyes. Stan. His mentor and friend. All he could think about was how much the man wanted to retire and spend time with his grandkids. "Is he all right?"

"He survived, but he's going to need surgery. So I need you here."

Jared turned to the doorway and found Dana standing there. She didn't look angry, just beautiful, and he couldn't help but remember last night in bed with her curled up against him. So trusting. He didn't deserve that trust because he was going to break her heart.

"I'll be there as soon as possible."

Dana could only watch as Jared packed his bag. He'd had very little in the way of clothes, at least until he had bought boots and more jeans. It still hadn't taken him long to gather it all together. The one thing he didn't pack was the navy blue suit he'd bought for their wedding. That gave her a glimmer of hope.

Her nervousness grew. "How long will you be gone?"

"Not sure," he answered. "Stan will be in the hospital until after his open-heart surgery. At least two weeks."

He turned around and studied her. "I'll be honest with you, Dana. I doubt he'll be bouncing back. That leaves me to run Burke Construction. And right now, we have several projects and completion dates to meet."

So you can leave Evan and me without a thought, she wanted to scream at him. "I understand. And I'm sorry about your friend. Evan and I will manage all right," she lied, knowing their relationship was over. Worse, she had to explain to Evan that Jared was leaving. "Just do me one favor and don't leave without talking with Evan."

Jarred crossed the room. "You really think I'd do that? You think it isn't killing me to leave that boy...to leave you? I told you from the first, Dana. I'm not cut out to be a family, but that doesn't mean that I don't care about you and Evan."

That was the problem—he cared too damn much. He cared more than he should for the woman whom he'd started to share a bed with.

Her emerald eyes looked pleadingly at him. He couldn't resist and he pulled her into his arms. "God, Dana. I don't have a choice. I have to go to Las Vegas."

"I know." A tear slid down her cheek and Jared brushed it away. "I just wish—"

He didn't want to hear her words. He was so torn that he couldn't weaken his resolve. He let his mouth coax hers into submission, letting her know of his desire for her, his want, but mostly his need. All too soon, he broke off the kiss and grabbed his bag off the bed and walked down the hall to Evan's room.

The boy was sitting at his desk and coloring. Jared stood there for a while, just trying to absorb the boy, wanting to keep the picture.

"Evan," he called.

The boy turned and smiled, then climbed off the chair and hurried to him. "Uncle Jared, look what I drew." He handed him a picture. Jared examined it closely. It looked like a horse and three stick people.

"That's us," Evan said. "You, me, Mom and Goldie. We are a family."

Family. Jared had hated the word when it came to the

Hastings. He'd never felt a part; now it was different. "It's very nice." He started to hand it back.

"No, I drew it for you," Evan insisted. "You keep it."

"I will." He looked at the boy. "Evan, I came in here because I have to tell you something. You know I have a construction business in Las Vegas."

The child nodded.

"Well, my boss got sick and I need to go there and help them finish the building."

He watched Evan's face drop. "But that's far away. I don't want you to go."

"It can't be helped, son."

"I don't care. I want you to stay here," he cried, and threw himself into Jared's arms and sobbed.

Jared hugged the boy to him, feeling like crying himself. "Hey, sport. I'll be back in a few weeks. By then you'll be riding Goldie like a champ."

The boy pulled back, wiping the tears off his face. "Will you come back and build me the fort you promised for my birthday?"

That was only two weeks away, Jared doubted that he could get things straightened out by then. And he didn't want to make the kid any false promises. "I'll try, son. If I can't be here, I'll call you."

Evan didn't like it, but he nodded. "'Kay."

"And you can call me." He went to the desk and wrote down the series of numbers to his cell phone. "If you need me, call."

The boy nodded, then hugged him. "I love you, Jared."

"I love you, too, Evan." He turned to find Dana standing in the doorway. Without a word, he moved past her and hurried down the steps.

Dana fought to rush after Jared and beg him to stay. What good would it do? He was determined to go. The pain was worse than anything she'd ever felt before.

She knew he had to go. After hearing the back door slam, she hurried downstairs.

Outside, Jared loaded his tools in the bed of his truck. After he finished the task, he went to the bunkhouse. Probably to say goodbye to Bert. A few minutes later, he came out and stood on the stoop and gazed out toward the pasture. It was as if he was taking a final look at the Lazy S. He turned toward the porch and paused. Dana's heart pounded, praying he'd come to her and promise that he would return. That he cared and wanted their marriage to be a real one.

Instead, he waved and climbed into his truck and drove off down the road, kicking up dust in his wake. Dana felt a tear run down her face and she brushed it off as he disappeared from view.

She knew in her heart that Jared Trager wasn't coming back.

Chapter Eleven

Jared had been gone five miserable days and six long, lonely nights. Worse, there hadn't been a word from him. Not even a quick phone call to tell her he'd made it to Las Vegas. Nothing.

Dana wasn't surprised. Jared had been honest with her. From the first, he'd told her that he didn't want anything permanent, that their so-called marriage was only temporary. Well, dammit, why did he have to treat her so special—be so loving? Why did he promise Evan that he'd always be there for him when he knew it was a lie? Wanting to protect her son, she'd made every excuse possible so Evan wouldn't know his uncle Jared had deserted him, that another man had walked away. Another man who didn't love her enough to stay.

From the kitchen, Dana heard a vehicle pull into the drive. She tried to hold back hope that it might be Jared as she went to the back door, but was disappointed to find it was Chance Randell coming up the walk.

"Afternoon, Dana." Her neighbor tipped his hat as he

climbed the steps. "You think I could have a word with you?"

Dana didn't feel like discussing business today or any day, but her solitude was worse.

"Come inside, it's cooler." She held open the wooden screen door, then led the way into the kitchen. She poured them both some iced tea as Chance pulled out a chair and straddled it.

She handed him the tea and he took a long, thirsty drink. "Thanks. That hit the spot. I've been working my cutters all morning."

She took a seat across from him. "What did you want to talk to me about?"

"First, I need to set the record straight," he began. "The day I came to help Jared with the horse corral, he had no idea I was going to suggest he join the Mustang Valley corporation."

Dana already knew that. "Well, it doesn't matter anymore because Jared is gone."

Chance frowned. "I know he's in Vegas, but he's coming back."

Hope sprang eternal. "Did he tell you that?"

"Not exactly, more like…he'd be gone a while."

Dana wasn't convinced, not after the argument they had. And not when he had the lure of Las Vegas and his dream. Besides, if Jared planned to come back, wouldn't he have called her?

"Well, I doubt it now, since our arrangement was never meant to be permanent." Her cheeks reddened in embarrassment. "Jared was only helping us get back on our feet and we're doing fine."

"I think Joy and I started out saying the same thing," Chance commented, trying to hide a smile.

"No, this is different. Jared's life is in Las Vegas."

Chance frowned. "He's also made a life here. I don't think he's the type of man to leave you high and dry. You're his wife and Evan is his nephew."

That didn't seem to matter to Jared, Dana thought, swallowing back her emotions. "Like I said, we're managing."

"Is that so?" Chance watched her closely. "If you weren't, would you ask a neighbor for help?"

"It's hard for me—" she straightened "—to take charity."

"We neighbors call it a helping hand. Not too long ago there were some people around here who didn't want anything to do with a Randell. That's hard on a man's pride. My brothers and I know what it's like to feel like a charity case. I'd never do that to anyone."

Dana saw the flash of pain in his eyes. She'd been too young back then to know all about the Randell story. She could only imagine what those young boys had to go through, no one wanting them, having to live down their father's sins.

"Back to that day, my offer to Jared was strictly a business deal," Chance began again. "Joy made me see it was a mistake not to approach you both. I'm sorry, Dana. I should have included you, too, in my idea."

Dana was surprised. "What idea?"

"Mustang Valley Guest Ranch needs a riding stable. Right now we don't have the horses or the room to board the number of mounts our guests need. We also want to include your section of land in the guest ranch. Thought you might also think about adding some cabins on your property."

He drew a breath and released it. "The only reason I approached Jared is that you and I hadn't had the best relationship over the past few years. I hope we can clear up this misunderstanding. Believe me, Dana, the Randells don't need any more land. Your strip of the valley land is yours. We only want to make sure it's protected along with the mustangs. That's the legacy that Hank wants to leave to us and future generations.

"So now I'm coming to you directly with the same offer—we want you to add your section of land to ours. Join our corporation and build your riding stable closer to the valley."

She couldn't believe what Chance was offering her. "But what if Jared doesn't return?"

Chance pursed his lips. "I don't know Jared that well, but what I do know is that he cares about you and Evan. But he's a Randell and he's going to be stubborn about admitting his feelings, so it might take a while for him to work it out." Chance grew serious. "Jared wasn't as lucky as the rest of us Randells. We had Hank to love us and keep us headed in the right direction. Jared's been pretty much alone most of his life and he might think that's all he deserves."

"But he has Evan…and me now."

Chance smiled. "I think he knows that, but as Joy would say, it takes a man a little longer to admit that he needs a good woman to share his life. So let Jared work some things out on his own. Then he'll be back. I bet my top quarter horse on it." Chance got up and placed his glass in the sink. "Take a few days and think over my offer—"

"I don't need time," Dana said, too excited to sit any longer. "I want to do it. At least the part about providing the saddle horses for the guest ranch." She didn't stop there. "Would you have a problem with me having my own students? Giving lessons to people other than your guests? I was thinking it would be easier for me if I keep all my mounts in one stable.'' She couldn't believe she was considering this.

Chance looked thoughtful. ''It'll be your business. We just need your services for our guests who want to ride. As long as you take care of the ranch guests, you can give riding lessons to anyone else who wants them. I'll give you a few days to think about it and then I'll call you. In the meantime, if you have any problems with anything let me know.''

''I will.'' Dana nodded, surprisingly not minding Chance's offer of help.

Chance stopped at the back door. ''By the way, there was an older man who stopped by the house this morning, asking for directions to your ranch. A stranger. Definitely not from around here. I wasn't crazy about him asking questions about you and Evan. Not to worry, I didn't tell him anything and sent him on his way.''

Who would be looking for her? She felt Chance's concern. ''Who was he?''

''Said his name was Graham Hastings.''

Dana's breath caught in her throat. She gasped.

Chance returned to her side. ''Do you know who he is?''

''He's Evan's grandfather. He wants to take my son away.''

Jared rested his head on his folded arms on top of the desk, trying to catch a nap. He'd only managed a few hours a night in the past ten days. He'd been working around the clock with three shifts trying to get the project done on time.

The good thing was they were going to make the deadline. But as soon as they finished this job, Burke Construction had another project about to start. Luckily he had a crackerjack crew that could handle the heavy load. Jared only wished he could. He remembered a time when he'd loved the continuous work. Not anymore. Maybe he was getting old.

Jared leaned back in his chair and thought about the auburn-haired woman who'd been a constant reminder of the life he'd only gotten a glimpse of. The short time he had with her had been like a dream. Maybe it was good he'd been called away, because it would have ended soon anyway. He'd already gone too far when he started sharing his bed with Dana. He muffled a groan, remembering the closeness they'd shared for just a few weeks. What man wouldn't get addicted to having a sexy, willing woman next to him in bed? His body stirred to life at the memory of the feel of Dana's hands on him.

The trailer door swung open and Jared sat up. Nate walked in. "Hey, Trager, there's a guy out here says he's family."

It had better not be Graham. "What's his name?"

"Randell."

Jared shot out of his chair just as Chance came through the door. Had something happened at the ranch? "Chance, what are you doing here? Is there a problem with Dana and Evan? Bert?"

"They're all okay. I'm here to talk some sense into you. And yes, there are problems. But they'd be solved if you were back in Texas where you belong." He looked around the small, messy construction trailer. "How can you stand this cramped space?"

"I don't usually work here," Jared said. "I work out at the site." He pointed to the two-story framed structure outside the door.

Chance shook his head. "Still the same thing. There's

too damn many people and cars in this town. How do you handle it?''

Jared leaned a hip on the edge of the desk and folded his arms. Even though he had only been gone a short time, he'd missed his brother's strong opinion. "I guess you get used to it."

"Why would you want to?"

Jared thought about it for a moment. The only thing he came up with was he'd never had a choice before. He had always gone where there was work. "Because the money is here."

"There's more in life than money, Jared. It took me a while to realize that, too. I guess you could say it was luck when Jack Randell ditched us kids and Hank took us in. Hank Barrett taught us that love of family was what mattered." Chance studied Jared for a long time. "How long is it going to take for you to realize that you belong in West Texas with your family?"

Those were sweet words to Jared's ears, but he was still afraid to dream. "I'm not like you, Cade and Travis. I don't have roots. I don't have a Hank to ground me."

"You have us. Your brothers. You have Dana…and Evan."

Something around Jared's heart tightened when he pictured Evan. He knew the boy needed him, and he wanted to be there for him. "I planned to call Evan on his birthday."

"My, aren't you generous? So much effort. I thought you promised your brother Marsh that you'd look after his son."

"I did. And I will. I just can't right now."

"Well, that's just too damn bad," Chance huffed. "Kids can't wait until we have the time for them. Before you know it, they're grown and they resent the hell out of you because you didn't give a damn about them.''

''I have responsibilities here.''

Chance shook his head. ''With that attitude maybe it would have been better if you had never stopped at the Lazy S.''

Jared had nothing to say that would answer that. He was hurting too bad. It wasn't that he didn't want Dana. He ached for her. He wanted to be the father that Evan deserved, but what if he failed at the job? What kind of example had he had?

''I'm not father material.''

''If you're thinking you're like your old man, forget it. I've seen you with Evan. You love that kid and you love Dana.''

Chance's words rung in his ears. He didn't want to think about feelings. All he knew was that he hadn't wanted to hurt Dana or Evan. But it looked like he had.

''I guess I wasted my time coming here.'' Chance walked toward the door, then stopped and looked over his shoulder at Jared. ''Just think about one thing. Think about another man in Dana's life—another man touching her, making love to her... Another man being a father to Evan.''

Jared clenched his fists, trying desperately to control his anger. Damn, but he wanted to hit something or someone.

Chance cocked an eyebrow. ''Eats at your gut, doesn't it? Good.'' He jerked open the door. ''One more thing. Remember when I said there was a problem? Graham Hastings is in San Angelo. He's been asking about his grandson.''

Jared stood up. ''He hasn't gotten to him, has he?''

''No, not yet.''

"Dammit, Chance, if he gets anywhere near the boy…"

Chance glared. "Then you better do something to protect your son."

When the door closed, Jared started after Chance, but stopped. Maybe he should call Graham. No, he wouldn't give the old man the satisfaction.

Jared began to pace. He had to keep his head. First, he couldn't run out on the job here. Stan had just gotten home from the hospital and Burke Construction was in the process of becoming Jared's obligation. But at the moment, his own responsibilities to the company were the last thing he cared about. His family was being threatened and thanks to him, Dana and Evan were all alone. Wasn't his main responsibility to his family?

Jared raked his hair with agitated fingers. She had to hate him. He'd let her down just like Marsh had. How could he go back to her and make her believe? He stopped. God. He loved Dana. His chest constricted as he closed his eyes and saw her pretty face. The freckles across her nose, her sparkling green eyes that seem to look right through to his soul. Her gentle touch that erased the years of loneliness. The sweet body she'd given so freely that he thought he'd die from the pleasure.

And in return, she asked nothing from him. Well, she had stolen something. His heart.

All at once the walls of the trailer seemed to be closing in on him. How could he have been so wrong? This wasn't the life he wanted. He knew now what he truly wanted. His family. Nothing else mattered but Dana and Evan.

He only prayed they still wanted him.

It was nearly midnight when Dana carried her glass of iced tea outside to the porch. She was dressed for bed, but far from sleepy. She hoped some quiet time alone would cure her insomnia. And tonight of all nights she needed her rest for the busy day tomorrow.

It was Evan's birthday and she had planned a party. It was going to be a small one, but thanks to Joy and the other Randells, Evan was going to have his special day.

Once seated on the padded glider, Dana tucked her bare feet under her as the crickets chirped through the silence. She took a sip of her tea and inhaled the scent of roses from the trellis next to the porch. She closed her eyes, wishing she could perk up—for her son's sake.

It had been two weeks and she had to face facts. Jared wasn't coming back. So she had to move on, and if she did, Evan would have to, as well. Tears burned her eyes as the familiar ache invaded her chest. She was trying, but so far nothing seemed to work. Nothing filled the big void in her life…in her son's life. As much as she wanted to despise Jared, she hadn't been able to summon the energy.

Brushing away the moisture from her cheeks, she looked up when she heard a vehicle coming down the road.

She tensed. Of course, Bert and Owen were in the bunkhouse so she wasn't alone. Her big concern was who would drop by at this hour, unless it was an emergency. The glare of the headlights blinded her momentarily as the truck swung into the drive. When Dana caught a flash of black, her pulse started racing. It was a Chevy extended cab. Jared's.

She froze as the vehicle finally came to a stop and her husband climbed out. With the help of the moonlight, her starved gaze moved over him as he started up the walk. His long legs were clad in jeans and a dark T-shirt molded itself to his broad chest and wide shoulders. The sound of his boots on the wooden steps kept in rhythm with the loud pounding of her heart. Finally he reached the porch and her.

Dana nervously twisted her mussed braid as she glanced down at her gown and robe. Lord, she wasn't even dressed.

"Hello, Dana. I'm glad you're up," Jared said as he walked across to her.

She didn't want to see him like this. He could at least have given a girl some warning. She finally found her voice. "What are you doing here?"

"I need to talk with you," he said.

She refused to hang around and let him break her heart all over again. No way. She stood up and caught sight of Owen as he came across the yard.

"Is everything okay, Dana?" the ranch hand called to her.

Before she could say anything, Jared spoke up. "Hey, Owen, it's just me. I drove all night to get here. Sorry I woke you."

"No problem. Good to have you home, Jared." Owen turned and walked away. Dana wanted to call him back, but it was better that he leave. This was a job she had to do.

She faced Jared. "If you need to pick up the rest of your things, be quick, and don't wake up Evan. I don't want you getting his hopes up. And don't worry about the loan money. If it's the last thing I do, I'll pay you back every cent." She started past him when he gripped her arm.

"I said, I need to talk to you, Dana, and it has nothing to do with money."

She raised her eyes to his. A bad idea, she realized as her throat tightened in longing.

"I made a lot of mistakes," he began. "But I never meant to hurt you and Evan."

"Would you stop?" She jerked away. "I don't need your pity, Jared Trager. I learned a long time ago to take care of myself. Not to depend on anyone. Evan and I managed just fine before you came. We'll make it just fine after you leave." She marched toward the door, fighting tears, praying she could get inside before she broke down.

"I won't be so lucky, Dana," he said softly. "I won't make it."

She paused, afraid to hope.

A little shaky, Jared took that walk toward her. "I thought everything I wanted was in Las Vegas. I was wrong. It wasn't until I was without you and Evan that I realized how lonely my life had been." He made a move to touch her. It nearly killed him to pull back. "Dana, I want to come back…and see if we can make our marriage work."

She turned around. Her green eyes glistened with tears and he hated that he caused it. "How can we do that, when you never wanted the responsibility of a family?"

She wasn't making this easy. "A man can change his mind. He can finally discover what's important. Maybe it took me longer than most, but I want to try…with you."

"For how long, Jared? How long before you get restless and want to leave again?"

"I'm never going to leave you."

She shook her head. "Yeah, I've heard that before."

Jared pulled her to him. "You haven't heard it from me," he breathed against her face. "So I'm telling you now. I want to be here with you—for you and Evan. I want to make a life for us.''

She turned away. "I can't do that, Jared," she whispered, and he could hear the pain in her voice. "I can't risk you hurting Evan again. You broke his heart when you left.''

"I know, and no one is sorrier than I am. Just give me a chance to make it up to him…to you.''

"Until you decide it's time to move on. No, Jared, I can't. I can't.'' She rushed into the house and closed the door. The click of the lock sounded so final to Jared.

Dejected, he turned and walked down the steps. So he'd been too late. She wouldn't take him back and he didn't blame her. He headed to the truck.

"So you just givin' up?" a voice called out. "I never took you for a quitter.''

Jared shot a look at the edge of the yard and discovered Bert standing there. He had on jeans and an undershirt.

"She won't take me back.''

The old man shook his head as he limped over to him. Bert leaned against the bed of the truck. "So you're just goin' to tuck your tail between your legs and head for the hills.''

"Well, what do you suggest I do?''

The man shrugged. "First, you have to find a way to cool her off just so she'll listen to your apology. You have to get on her good side.''

"I'll take any side as long as I can talk to her.''

The old foreman smacked his hand against his leg. "That's what I want to hear, son. Now, what's that girl's one weakness?" he asked, then raised a hand in warning. "Be careful. You fail this one, and I'll throw you off the place myself.''

Jared found himself smiling. "Evan.''

He nodded. "Now, you convince Dana how much the boy means to you. How much you want all of you to be a family. Guaranteed, you get the child on your side, then you'll soon have the mother."

"You think so?"

"The fact that the girl loves you something fierce doesn't hurt."

"Dana loves me?"

Bert nodded again. "And I wouldn't be wastin' my time with you if I didn't think you loved them both more than your own life. You couldn't help it if you were a little slow on discovering that part," he murmured.

"I *do* love Dana."

"Tell her, not me. And you better spend your time figuring out a plan to convince her."

Jared was already way ahead of him. "I think I have just the thing. Would you mind if I stayed in the bunkhouse tonight? I have a lot work to do by morning."

"Maybe, if you tell me what you're gonna do."

Jared grabbed his duffel bag and toolbox from the truck bed and started off to the bunkhouse. "Gladly, but you and Owen have to help me with Evan's surprise."

Chapter Twelve

The next morning came too soon as far as Dana was concerned, but she didn't waste any time. She had too much to do for Evan's birthday party. Six children would be coming. Four were Randells—toddlers Elisa Mae, Katie Rose, James Henry and also ten-year-old Brandon. Evan also had invited two friends, Matt and Michael, from his Sunday school class.

Then there were the adults: Chance and Joy, Abby and Cade, Josie and Travis Randell. Even Ella and Hank were coming. Except for Bert and Owen, Dana would be the only person who wasn't part of a couple.

She turned her thoughts to last night and Jared's return. Today could have been so different, if only she'd asked him to stay. Her heart ached at the thought of him not being in her life. It shocked her how much she'd come to rely on him. How much she'd come to love him.

Last night she'd wanted desperately to call him back, to fall into his arms, but in the long run both she and Evan would only be hurt. She couldn't let Jared back into their lives only to have him leave again. And she would do anything to protect her son from any more pain and disappointment.

Dana went downstairs to the kitchen where she found Evan dressed and waiting for her. By the expression on his face, he didn't look like he was ready for a big party today.

"Hello, sweetheart. How's the birthday boy?"

Evan shrugged. "I'm okay."

"What would you like for your special birthday breakfast?"

Another shrug. "I'm not hungry."

She pulled out a chair and sat down next to him. "You know what happens to a birthday boy who doesn't smile? He gets tickled!" She went for his ribs and realized that he had tears in his eyes.

She stopped. "Evan, tell me what's wrong."

"He promised, Mom. Jared promised he'd be here for my birthday." The child began to sob against her shoulder.

She hugged him to her, fighting her own tears. "I know, honey. I'm sorry. But sometimes things can't be helped." She felt guilty that she'd been the one to send Jared away. But in the long run, she'd had to do what was best for all of them. "There'll be lots of other people coming today. All the Randells and their kids. And Chance is going to bring his horse, Roughneck, and show you all his tricks. There'll be games and presents. Oh, and Bert and I have a real big present for you."

The child raised his head and wiped his tears away. "I don't care. I only want Uncle Jared."

So did she. "It's pretty big and way cool."

That caught his interest. "How big?"

"So big, I couldn't bring it into the house. We've been

hiding it in the barn." Dana had been tickled when Bert found a secondhand children's saddle. He'd spent weeks cleaning and repairing the tack until it looked new. "How about we go out there right now and have a look?" she asked.

When he nodded, she said, "You go ahead and find Bert, I'll be right out."

"'Kay," Evan said and took off.

As soon as the door slammed, Dana's own tears fell. "Damn you, Jared Trager. Why did you ever have to come here? Why did you ever have to let us love you?"

Suddenly Evan called out. "Mom! Come outside. Hurry!"

Dana rushed to the door as her son ran up on the porch. "Evan? What's the matter?"

"He's back," he cried, waving for her to follow him. He scurried down the steps and ran to the side of the house.

"Evan, wait." Dana hurried after him around the corner of the house and stopped suddenly when she spotted what Evan was pointing at. Jared Trager up on a ladder wielding a paintbrush over the faded wood siding. By the looks of the large glossy white section painted, he'd been at it for a while.

"Hi, Uncle Jared," Evan called out as he waved.

"Hey, it's the birthday boy."

"I'm five today."

"I know," Jared said as he laid his paintbrush across the bucket and wiped his hands on the rag hanging from his pocket.

Dana couldn't take her eyes off the man as he slowly descended the twelve-foot ladder. He wore only jeans and his work boots, his bare chest glistening in the morning sun. Her pulse started as she recalled a few other mornings, with him lying next to her.... She shook away the thought.

"What are you doing here?" she asked, trying to work up some anger.

Jared placed his hands on his hips. "I realized I have a lot of things around here that I need to finish."

Dana didn't want him finishing anything. "You've already done enough. Don't you need to get back to Las Vegas, to your construction company?"

"There's no hurry." His gaze locked with hers, and she had trouble breathing. "I don't break promises." He turned to Evan. "And I came back for your birthday."

Evan's eyes widened. "You're coming to my party?"

Jared smiled. "Wouldn't miss it. And I brought you a special present."

"You got me a present?"

Jared nodded. "Maybe if you ask your mother she'll let you open it now."

Both Jared and Evan looked at her. What choice did she have? The man wasn't playing fair. "I guess one wouldn't hurt."

"Oh, boy." Evan cheered.

"It's over there on the deck." Jared pointed and they both watched as the child ran off.

Dana glared at Jared. "I don't know what you're trying to pull, but I don't like it. Not when my son could end up hurt."

Jared knew he still had a lot of convincing to do. "I'm not going to hurt Evan. I love the boy. I'm trying to tell you that you both matter to me. I want a life with you and Evan."

"Don't, Jared." She stopped him. "We went over this last night. You don't want to stay here." Tears formed in her eyes. "Sooner or later you'll leave us. Please, give him your present and make an excuse and leave."

She turned away and Jared stuffed his hands into his pockets to keep from pulling her into his arms.

"I don't think it's Evan that you're worried about, Dana. I think it's you who are afraid. You care about me, or you would have never come to my bed and let me make love to you."

When she didn't respond, he gripped her arm and made her look at him. "And if you don't think what we have is special, or that I don't love you more than my next breath, then I guess I *am* wasting my time." He released her and started toward Evan. He took a deep breath trying to hang on to his control. He needed to keep it together for the boy's sake.

Jared grabbed his shirt off the deck and slipped it on. This wasn't working out the way he'd hoped. Although it felt as if his heart had been ripped from his chest, he plastered a smile on his face and watched Evan rip the paper off his birthday gift then lifted the lid to reveal a miniature tool belt.

"Wow." Evan held it up. "It's just like yours."

"It sure is," Jared said. "I had it made specially for you."

The boy hugged him. "Thanks, Uncle Jared."

"You're welcome," he managed, swallowing the rush of emotions. He took the belt from the boy and draped it around his narrow waist. "Now, there are some tools that go in here, but I'll put those in when we're working on something. You have to promise not to use them unless I'm with you."

"I promise." He smiled. "Look, Mom, it's cool."

"It sure is." Dana smiled. "Evan, I need to talk with Bert. Will you stay here with Jared a few minutes?"

Dana turned and hurried off to the barn, barely making it inside before she fell apart. She ended up in Sweet Brandy's stall, taking her solace from the affectionate filly.

"I take it you didn't accept Jared's offer?"

Dana looked up to see Bert. "What are you talking about?"

"Your husband is out there and you're in here crying your eyes out."

"I'm not crying and Jared was never really my husband." Dana turned away so she didn't have to look Bert in the eye.

"Girl, you know better than to lie. You two may have gotten married for different reasons, but there for a while I hadn't seen you so happy in a long time. And that man is the cause of it. He's the cause of your son's happiness, too."

"But he's leaving us."

"How do you know that? Didn't he say that he loved you and the boy?"

She nodded. "Words are easy. He left us just like Marshall did."

The old man limped to the stall gate and opened it. "There's one difference. Jared came back. Sweetheart, you can't make him keep paying for his brother's sins. If I've ever seen anyone who needs a family, that man does."

Dana was afraid to hope. "He'll always be pulled back to Las Vegas. He has his business there."

Bert frowned, emphasizing the lines on his face. "He didn't tell you?"

"Tell me what?"

"Jared backed out of the deal. He didn't buy the company."

Dana gasped. "But it's what he wanted. It was his dream."

The foreman pushed his hat back. "Funny thing about dreams... They aren't very important if you don't have someone to share them with. Jared's been looking for a place to belong. His dream is a family."

Another flood of tears threatened as Dana realized the risk Jared took to come to her. And she'd pushed him away. Made him think she didn't want him.

"Oh, Bert," she gasped, and the filly flinched. "I've been so wrong, I have to tell him...." Dana stepped out of the stall.

Bert grinned and waved. "You go on, girl, I'll handle Sweet Brandy."

Dana ran out of the barn and across the yard. Breathing hard, she rounded the house but didn't see Jared or Evan. Then she heard laughter and located the two in a grove of trees next to a stack of lumber.

She slowed her pace as she came up to them. Her son saw her first. "Look, Mom." He held out a piece of paper. "It's a fort. Uncle Jared and me are gonna build it. Together."

Jared stared into her eyes. "If it's okay with your mother."

Dana wanted to rush into his arms. Thank him for loving her son, praying he still loved her. "It's fine with me."

"Yippee! I'm gonna go and show Bert and Owen my tool belt!" Evan started off toward the barn.

Dana let her son go, her gaze never leaving Jared's face. Suddenly she was trembling, wanting him to reassure her. But how could she ask him to put himself on the line again, when she'd kept pushing him away?

"You sold your business?"

He looked surprised, then nodded. "I realized it wasn't what I really wanted."

"But it was your dream."

He shrugged. "Dreams change."

"What's your dreams now?"

"I don't think you want to hear them."

She came closer, so close she felt his heat and inhaled the familiar intoxicating scent of him. "I do," she breathed. "I wasn't ready to listen yesterday, but I am now."

"All right. I want a family. Kids." He glanced around. "I want a place like this." His eyes met hers. "Most of all, I want you and Evan in my life."

Excitement poured through her. "Did you mean what you said earlier?"

Jared knew exactly what Dana was asking. "Yes, Dana, I meant every word. I love you."

When she gasped, he enfolded her in his arms and drew her against him. "I can't live without you," he continued. "You've gotten into my heart. *You* are my heart. You and Evan."

"Oh, Jared, I love you, too. So much." She closed her eyes, momentarily. "I was afraid that—"

He stopped her words when his mouth captured hers in a hungry kiss that he hoped relayed his gratitude for her trust and love. They clung to each other like a lifeline, barely controlling their desire.

"Tell me again," he asked as he cupped her face.

"I love you."

He closed his eyes and pressed his forehead against hers. "Ah, Dana, I love you so much. I thought if I went back to Las Vegas I could forget you and Evan. It only made me realize what an empty life that I truly had there."

"But you wanted to buy the construction company." She still couldn't believe it.

"It didn't mean as much to me as you and Evan."

"Oh, Jared, but you loved it."

"I love being a carpenter. And I think I'll have plenty of that to do around here. I'm going to make the Lazy S a showplace again. And after that I don't think I'll have trouble finding work around San Angelo." Jared held Dana to him, loving the feel of her body against his. "If you're worried about me being able to support you, don't. I still have plenty in my trust fund."

"I never cared about your money."

He gave her a wink. "I know, you had designs on my body."

She laughed, but it quickly died. "I've been so lonely since you've been gone."

He pulled her closer to him. "Not as lonely as I've been. I missed your body tucked up against mine. I miss the soft sounds you make when I touch you...love you. Oh, yes, I've definitely been away from you too long." His mouth closed over hers in another hungry kiss.

They broke apart when they heard the sound of a car coming up the road. A long, black town car. Dread washed over him.

"Who is it, Jared?"

"Graham Hastings." He wished he could erase the worry in her eyes. "You stay here, Dana. I'll handle it."

He walked to the car just as a white-haired man climbed out. Jared stood in front of his father, blocking his path. "What are you doing here?"

"Did you think I wouldn't find out about my grandson?" Graham said. "I plan to be a part of his life."

Not if Jared could help it. "Marsh didn't even want

you to know about Evan, let alone have you in his life. Neither do I. I'm his stepfather and I plan to adopt him.''

"I can give him so much more than you can.''

Jared's fists clenched. "It always comes down to the money, doesn't it, GH? Evan doesn't need your money. He needs a father who will be there for him. And I will. So you can leave now.''

"You really are a bastard.'' Graham reached into his pocket, pulled out a photograph and handed it to Jared. "But you're not Jack Randell's only one. It seems he's spread his seed all over the West. There are two more out there.''

Jared fought to show a reaction. "Why is it so important?''

"Years ago I hired a private investigator to find out about your mother's...indiscretion with Randell. Couldn't have him showing up and trying to get money. It seemed I never had to worry. Jack Randell didn't want any of his...kids.''

Jared didn't want to hear anymore. "Well, you've said your piece, so you can leave now. I'm Evan's stepfather and if possible I'll do everything to keep you away from him.''

Just then Evan came out of the barn. Graham's attention darted to the boy and Jared thought he saw longing in the old man's eyes. Then it disappeared and Graham climbed back into the car and drove off.

Dana rushed to Jared. "Don't worry,'' he assured her. "He's not going to take Evan away. I promise.'' He kissed her.

"Yuck, you guys are kissing.''

Jared tucked the photo into his pocket. "You have a problem with me kissing your mom?''

Evan shook his head. "No, 'cause she's happy when

you kiss her.'' He came closer. ''Are you gonna live here and be my dad?''

Jared crouched down. ''Yes, I'm going to live here. And if it's okay I'd like to be your dad.''

Evan glanced at his mother, then at Jared. ''You love us?''

''Yes, I love you and your mother very much.''

Evan threw himself at Jared. ''I love you, too, Dad.''

There was no other feeling in the world like a child's loving arms. For the first time ever, Jared knew he'd found what he'd been looking for.

Suddenly a caravan of cars moved down the road. ''Looks like the party is about to start,'' Jared said.

''Oh, no,'' Dana cried as the Randells began filing out of the cars. ''I have so much to do before I'm ready.''

Jared pulled his wife back into his arms. ''Don't worry. We're all family.'' He sure liked the sound of that.

Epilogue

Dana loved her life.

She sat atop Scout, looking down at Mustang Valley. A herd of wild ponies were contentedly grazing in the high grass, not paying one bit of attention to the many tourists who'd ridden along the ridge to see them.

Just two weeks ago, Chance and Jared had finished the horse corral a short distance away, so as not to disturb the natural look of the valley. In the mornings, Dana took ranch guests on trail rides, then afternoons were reserved for her own group and private lessons. Her business was booming.

Things weren't stopping there. Over the winter, Jared would be building six cabins on their part of the valley. By next spring they should be ready for guests. That wasn't all. Chance had agreed to breed one of his studs with her bay, Sweet Brandy. And Dana already had people interested in the future foal. Right now, she had Lazy S's roundup in a few weeks, but she wasn't worried about finding help. The entire Randell family had already volunteered.

Dana couldn't believe the summer was nearly over, and on Monday, Evan would start kindergarten. That was the reason for the picnic in the valley. Everyone rode in on horseback, including Evan on Goldie, for one last party for all the kids.

One big family. And the Randells included Jared as a part of it, along with her and Evan. And that family just kept on growing. Dana touched her stomach. In so many ways.

She climbed down from her horse and walked to the stream.

"What are you smiling about?"

She turned to find that Jared had ridden up. He jumped down and sauntered toward her. Over the last months on the ranch, Jared had taken to his new life as if he'd always lived here, dressed in his Wrangler jeans and light-blue Western shirt, along with his slow easy gait and even the tilt to his Stetson. Her breath quickened just looking at him.

"Hello, cowboy," she said. "I'm just counting my blessings. I have so many."

"We both have." He came up behind her, wrapped his arms around her middle and together they watched as the kids rode by on the other side of the stream.

Evan sat straight in the saddle, riding behind his new cousin, Brandon. Owen was keeping a keen eye on them both. The young ranch hand had decided to stay and go to college in San Angelo so he'd be able to work part-time at the Lazy S.

Hank Barrett brought up the rear of the group as he rode alongside little Katie Rose on her pony. Recovering from knee surgery, Bert wasn't able to ride yet. He still walked with a cane, but that didn't slow him down. He was in charge of grilling the hot dogs for the kids up at the cabin on the ridge.

"Life can't be any more perfect than this," Dana breathed, feeling so safe and loved in her husband's arms.

When Jared didn't respond, Dana looked over her shoulder and saw the faraway look in his eyes. She knew what had been bothering him. Graham Hastings's revelation about the existence of more Randell brothers. "Are you second-guessing your decision?"

"Yeah, I just hope I did the right thing by sending that photograph off to the Gentrys."

"How could you not?" she asked. "Don't they have a right to know who their father is? What they choose to do with it is their business."

He nodded. "I guess. I just feel bad because I haven't said anything to the others." He shook his head. "Two more brothers. Twins."

"And you will tell Chance and the others, if and when you hear from the Gentrys."

"Of course," Jared agreed, then leaned down and kissed her briefly. Too briefly, as far as Dana was concerned. She loved being with family, but wished they had some alone time right now. Not that she and Jared hadn't sneaked off to the valley before and made love.

"This is a special place," he said, breaking into her thoughts. "I felt it the first time I ever rode in here. Chance said that he and his brothers felt they were misfits just like the mustangs."

"Do you feel like a misfit?"

"Not any longer." He hugged her. "I found everything that I've ever wanted right here. You and Evan are my family."

Dana couldn't contain her excitement any longer and

turned in his arms. "I hope you don't mind expanding our family." She reached up and placed a kiss on his lips. "I'm pregnant."

Jared couldn't hide his shock. A flood of feelings rushed through him as he moved his hand over his wife's flat stomach. There was a new life inside. His child. "Oh, God, Dana." He kissed her, kissed her again and again. "Are you sure?"

She nodded. "As of this morning."

"A baby," he breathed. His eyes met her beautiful green gaze. "I love you, Dana Shayne Trager. So much." His mouth closed over hers, wanting to tell her what words couldn't relay. That he'd finally found peace and love. And the one place he'd been searching for. A place where he belonged.

* * * * *

It's romantic comedy with a kick
(in a pair of strappy pink heels)!

Introducing

HARLEQUIN flipside

"It's chick-lit with the romance and happily-ever-after ending that Harlequin is known for."
—*USA TODAY* bestselling author Millie Criswell, author of *Staying Single*, October 2003

"Even though our heroine may take a few false steps while finding her way, she does it with wit and humor."
—Dorien Kelly, author of *Do-Over*, November 2003

Launching October 2003.
Make sure you pick one up!

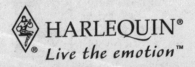

HARLEQUIN®
Live the emotion™

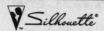

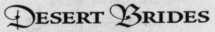

If you enjoyed what you just read,
then we've got an offer you can't resist!

Take 2 bestselling love stories FREE!

Plus get a FREE surprise gift!

Clip this page and mail it to Silhouette Reader Service™

IN U.S.A.
3010 Walden Ave.
P.O. Box 1867
Buffalo, N.Y. 14240-1867

IN CANADA
P.O. Box 609
Fort Erie, Ontario
L2A 5X3

YES! Please send me 2 free Silhouette Romance® novels and my free surprise gift. After receiving them, if I don't wish to receive anymore, I can return the shipping statement marked cancel. If I don't cancel, I will receive 6 brand-new novels every month, before they're available in stores! In the U.S.A., bill me at the bargain price of $3.34 plus 25¢ shipping and handling per book and applicable sales tax, if any*. In Canada, bill me at the bargain price of $3.80 plus 25¢ shipping and handling per book and applicable taxes**. That's the complete price and a savings of at least 10% off the cover prices—what a great deal! I understand that accepting the 2 free books and gift places me under no obligation ever to buy any books. I can always return a shipment and cancel at any time. Even if I never buy another book from Silhouette, the 2 free books and gift are mine to keep forever.

215 SDN DNUM
315 SDN DNUN

Name	(PLEASE PRINT)	
Address	Apt.#	
City	State/Prov.	Zip/Postal Code

* Terms and prices subject to change without notice. Sales tax applicable in N.Y.
** Canadian residents will be charged applicable provincial taxes and GST.
    All orders subject to approval. Offer limited to one per household and not valid to
    current Silhouette Romance® subscribers.
    ® are registered trademarks of Harlequin Books S.A., used under license.

SROM02   ©1998 Harlequin Enterprises Limited

SILHOUETTE *Romance*®

COMING NEXT MONTH

#1684 LOVE, YOUR SECRET ADMIRER—Susan Meier
Marrying the Boss's Daughter
Sarah Morris's makeover turned a few heads—including Matt Burke's, her sexy boss! But Matt's life plan didn't include romance. Tongue-tied and jealous, he tried to help Sarah discover her secret admirer's identity, but would he realize *he'd* been secretly admiring her all along?

#1685 WHAT A WOMAN SHOULD KNOW—Cara Colter
Tally Smith wanted a stable home for her orphaned nephew—and that meant marriage. Enter JD Turner, founder of the "Ain't Getting Married, No Way Never Club"—and Jed's biological father. Tally only thought it fair to give the handsome, confirmed bachelor the first shot at being a daddy…!

#1686 TO KISS A SHEIK—Teresa Southwick
Desert Brides
Heart-wounded single father Sheik Fariq Hassan didn't trust beautiful women, so hired nanny Crystal Rawlins disguised her good looks. While caring for his children, she never counted on Fariq's smoldering glances and knee-weakening embraces. But could he forgive her deceit when he saw the real Crystal?

#1687 WHEN LIGHTNING STRIKES TWICE—Debrah Morris
Soulmates
Joe Mitchum was a thorn in Dr. Mallory Peterson's side—then an accident left his body inhabited by her former love's spirit. Unable to tell Mallory the truth, the new Joe set out to change her animosity to adoration. But if he didn't succeed soon their souls would spend eternity apart….

#1688 RANSOM—Diane Pershing
Between a robbery, a ransom and a renegade cousin, Hallie Fitzgerald didn't have time for Marcus Walcott, the good-looking—good-kissing!—overprotective new police chief. So why was he taking a personal interest in her case? Any why was *she* taking such a personal interest in *him*?!

#1689 THE BRIDAL CHRONICLES—Lissa Manley
Jilted once, Ryan Cavanaugh had no use for wealthy women and no faith in love. But the lovely Anna Sinclair seemed exactly as she appeared—a hardworking wedding dress designer. Could their tender bond break through the wall around Ryan's heart…and survive the truth about Anna's secret identity?

SRCNM0803